"Lean your head against me and relax," Cal whispered.

Relax? With her cheek pressed against the soft cotton of his shirt, the steady beat of his heart beneath her ear? With the faint scent of his aftershave filling her nostrils? With the angle of his jaw brushing against her forehead, the faint end-of-day stubble creating a sensuous texture against her skin? He must be kidding!

But as they swung gently back and forth and dusk slowly deepened, she did relax. Cal knew she was afraid, just as he was, and he understood her caution. But he also knew— in fact, was even beginning to hope—that perhaps their fears were groundless. And before they left the mountains, he intended to find out.

Books by Irene Hannon

Love Inspired

Home for the Holidays #6
A Groom of Her Own #16
A Family To Call Her Own #25
It Had To Be You #58
One Special Christmas #77
The Way Home #112

*Vows

IRENE HANNON

has been a writer for as long as she can remember. This prolific author of romance novels for both the inspirational and traditional markets began her career at age ten, when she won a story contest conducted by a national children's magazine. Today, in addition to penning her heartwarming stories of love and faith, Irene keeps quite busy with her "day job" in corporate communications. In her "spare" time, she enjoys performing in community musical theater productions.

Irene and her husband, Tom—whom she describes as "my own romantic hero"—make their home in St. Louis, Missouri.

The Way Home
Irene Hannon

Love Inspired®

Published by Steeple Hill Books™

STEEPLE HILL BOOKS

Steeple
Hill™

ISBN 0-373-87118-X

THE WAY HOME

Copyright © 2000 by Irene Hannon Gottlieb

Visit us at www.steeplehill.com

Printed in U.S.A.

Not as man sees does God see, because man sees the appearance, but the Lord looks into the heart.

—*1 Samuel* 16:7

To Tom—my friend, my hero, my love...always

Chapter One

"There's your man!"

Amy Winter turned in the direction her cameraman was pointing and quickly scanned the group of people milling about in front of the courthouse.

"Where?"

"Straight ahead. Tall, dark hair, gray suit, intimidating. Carrying a black briefcase."

It took Amy only a moment to spot Cal Richards. "Intimidating" was right. As he strode purposefully through the group of people clustered on the sidewalk and headed toward the door, his bearing communicated a very clear message: "Back off." But clear or not, it was a message Amy intended to ignore. She took a deep breath and tightened her grip on the microphone.

"Okay, Steve. Let's go."

Without waiting for a reply, she headed toward her quarry and planted herself directly in his path.

Cal Richards didn't notice her until he was only a couple of feet away. Even then, he simply frowned, gave her a distracted glance and, without pausing, made a move to step around her. Except that she moved, too.

This time he looked right at her, and their gazes collided for one brief, volatile moment that made Amy's breath catch in her throat. The man had eyes that simultaneously assessed, calculated, probed—and sent an odd tingle up her spine. But before she had time to dwell on her unsettling reaction, his gaze moved on, swiftly but thoroughly sweeping over her stylish shoulder-length light brown hair, vivid green eyes and fashionably short skirt before honing in on the microphone in her hand and the cameraman behind her. His frown deepened, and the expression in his eyes went from merely annoyed to cold.

"Excuse me. I have work to do." The words were polite. The tone was not.

Amy's stomach clenched and she forced herself to take a deep breath. "So do I. And I was hoping you'd help me do it." Though she struggled to maintain an even tone, she couldn't control the slight tremor that ran through her voice. And that bothered her. She resented the fact that this stranger, with one swift look, could disrupt the cool, professional demeanor she'd worked so hard to perfect.

"I don't give interviews."

"I just have a couple of questions. It will only take a minute of your time."

"I don't have a minute. And I don't give inter-

views,'' he repeated curtly. ''Now, if you'll excuse—''

''Look, Mr. Richards, this trial is going to get publicity whether you cooperate or not,'' she interrupted,
willing her voice to remain steady. ''But as the assistant prosecuting attorney, you could add a valuable
perspective to the coverage.''

Cal expelled an exasperated breath. ''Look,
Ms....'' He raised an eyebrow quizzically.

''Winter. Amy Winter.'' She added the call letters
of her station.

''Ms. Winter. As I said before, I don't give interviews. Period. Not before, not during, not after a trial.
So you'll save us both a lot of trouble if you just
accept that right now. Trust me.''

Before she could protest, he neatly sidestepped her,
covered the distance to the courthouse door in a few
long strides and disappeared inside.

Amy stared after him in frustration, then turned to
Steve, who gave her an I-told-you-so shrug.

''Okay, okay, you warned me,'' she admitted with
an irritated sigh.

''Cal Richards has a reputation for never bending
the rules—his own or the law's. Everyone in the news
game knows that. Did you see anyone else even *try*
to talk to him?''

Steve was right. The other reporters in front of the
courthouse, most longtime veterans of the Atlanta
news scene, hadn't even approached the assistant
prosecuting attorney. They'd obviously learned a lesson she had yet to master after only six months in
town. Then again, she wasn't sure she *wanted* to learn

that lesson. If she was ever going to win the anchor spot she'd set her sights on, and ultimately a network feature slot, she had to find a way to make her coverage stand out. This story had potential. And getting Cal Richards's cooperation would be a coup that could boost her up at least a couple of rungs on the proverbial career ladder.

She turned once more to gaze thoughtfully at the door he had entered. Maybe Steve was right. Maybe the assistant prosecuting attorney wouldn't bend. Then again, maybe he would. And until she tried everything she could think of to induce a change of heart, she wasn't about to let Cal Richards off the hook.

Cal closed the door behind him, tossed his briefcase on the couch and wearily loosened his tie. The first day of jury selection had been frustrating and largely unproductive. Which was about what he'd expected, given the high-profile nature of this trial. Whenever a public figure had a run-in with the law, it was big news. Especially when that public figure was someone like Jamie Johnson, a well-liked sports hero, and the charge was so explosive—manslaughter. If any average citizen had been involved in a drunk-driving accident that left a pedestrian dead, they'd throw the book at him. But Jamie Johnson had public sentiment on his side. And since the victim was a homeless drifter, his death was being treated as no great loss.

Cal didn't see it that way. Manslaughter was manslaughter, as far as he was concerned. It didn't matter who the victim was. But Johnson was going to walk unless they came up with a rock-solid witness. Though the sports hero didn't dispute the drunk-driving charge, he claimed that the victim had stepped off the curb and into his path. And at the moment, it was his word against no one's. With his clean-cut good looks and apparent sincerity and remorse, he had the public eating out of his hand.

But he was guilty as sin, and Cal knew it deep in his gut. Johnson had had other minor run-ins with the law, was known to be a drinker, had demonstrated his irresponsibility in any number of ways the police were well aware of. Unfortunately, none of that was admissible as evidence.

Cal jammed his hands into his pockets and walked over to the window of his apartment. There were many things he liked about his job. The harsh reality of this kind of trial, where the odds of seeing justice done were minuscule, wasn't one of them. He would do his best, of course. He always did. But he'd been in this business long enough to learn that no matter how high your ideals were when you started, disillusion was your legacy. There were just too many instances where the "little guy," for lack of money or power, was shortchanged by the law. Cal worked hard to keep that from happening, and sometimes he won. That was what kept him going—knowing that in at least a few instances justice had been served because of his efforts. It was a deeply satisfying experience, but it happened too rarely.

Cal looked down at the glittering lights of the city and drew a long, slow breath, willing the tension in his shoulders to ease. It was a pretty view, one that his infrequent visitors always admired. But it wasn't home. Never would be. And, as usual, it did nothing to help him relax.

So instead he closed his eyes and pictured the evening mist on the blue-hued mountains outside his grandmother's cabin in Tennessee. He could almost feel the fresh breeze on his face, smell the faint, woodsy aroma of smoke curling from distant chimneys, hear the whisper of the wind in the pine trees and the call of the birds. As he let the remembered beauty seep into his soul, his mind gradually grew still and he was filled with a sense of peace.

When at last Cal opened his eyes, he felt better. Calmer. He'd lived in cities for almost half of his thirty-four years, but only Gram's cabin fit the definition of "home." It was still his refuge, the place he went when he couldn't handle the impersonal, fast-paced city anymore, when the frustration became too intense, when he needed to regain perspective. And he'd been going there a lot lately. Even after all these years, he felt like a stranger in the sterile environment of steel and concrete. Only in the mountains was he able to ease the growing restlessness in his soul.

But how could he ever explain that to his father? he asked himself dispiritedly for the thousandth time. Cal raked his fingers through his hair and sighed. Jack Richards would never understand. All his life, all the years he'd labored as a tenant farmer, he'd wanted a better life for his only offspring. And "better" to him meant an office job, a lucrative career, life in the big city. He'd instilled that same dream in his son, though it wasn't a dream Cal had taken to naturally. Unlike his father, he'd always loved the land. But somewhere along the way his father had convinced him that his destiny lay elsewhere, far from the blue-hazed Smoky Mountains. And the day Cal graduated from law school with an enviable, big-city job offer in his pocket, his destiny had seemed settled, his "success" assured.

In the intervening years, however, he'd begun to realize that deep inside he had never really shared his father's dream. The mountains called to him more and more strongly as the years passed. And it was a call he was finding harder and harder to ignore, especially on days like this. Yet how could he walk away from the life he'd built for himself, throw away all the long hours he'd invested in his career in Atlanta? Frustrating as it often was, there were also moments of deep satisfaction when he was able to help someone who really *needed* his help, who might be lost in the system without his intervention. That was why he had gone into law, why he still enjoyed it. And as he took on more and more responsibility, he would be in a position to do even more to further the cause of justice. It somehow seemed wrong to even *consider* leaving a job where he could be such an instrument for good. And further compounding the situation was his father. How could he disappoint the man who had worked so hard to give him a better life?

With an impatient shake of his head, Cal turned away from the window. He'd been wrestling with this dilemma for months, praying for guidance, but resolution was still nowhere in sight. And until his prayers were answered, he'd simply have to maintain the status quo. At least until his patience ran out. Which might not be too far down the road, he thought ruefully as he headed toward the kitchen.

The red light was blinking on his answering machine as he passed, indicating three messages, and he paused. Fortunately, his unlisted number kept crank calls and solicitations at bay. Only his close business associates, family and a few select friends were privy to his private line.

Despite the protest of his stomach, Cal deferred dinner for yet another few minutes. He straddled a stool at the counter, pulled a notepad toward him and punched Play.

The first two messages were easily dispensed with. The third was more disturbing.

"Mr. Richards, this is Amy Winter. We met this morning at the courthouse. I don't like to bother people at home, but I'm not having much luck connecting with you at your office, and I really would like to continue our discussion. As I told you, I'm covering the Johnson trial and your input would add a valuable perspective to the coverage. I realize, of course, that you can't discuss the trial in any detail, but perhaps you can suggest an angle I might investigate, or offer some other insights that would be helpful. Let me give you my work number and my home number…"

As she proceeded to do so, Cal's frown deepened. He didn't like reporters in general, and he especially didn't like pushy reporters. Which was exactly the category Amy Winter fit into. How in the world had she managed to get his unlisted number? And did she really think he'd return this call when he'd ignored both of the messages she'd left at his office earlier in the day?

Resolutely he punched the erase button. Obviously she was new on this beat or she'd know that his "no comment" meant exactly that. But she'd learn. In the meantime, if she continued to call his home number, he could always file a harassment complaint. He hoped it wouldn't come to that, but he didn't have time to play games. Sooner or later she'd get that message.

Apparently it was going to be "later," Cal thought resignedly when he spotted the persistent reporter on the courthouse steps the next morning. At least she'd left the cameraman back at the station this time, he noted.

"Good morning, Mr. Richards."

She sounded a bit breathless as she fell into step beside him, and he glanced over at her. The chilly, early-spring air had brought a becoming flush to her cheeks, and her jade-colored jacket complemented the startling green of her eyes. She was a very attractive woman, he realized. Then again, that seemed to be a prerequisite for broadcast news. As far as he was concerned, TV stations would be better off if they paid more attention to solid reporting skills and real news and less to cosmetics and sensationalism. He picked up his pace.

"If this keeps up, I'll have to wear my running shoes next time," she complained breathlessly, trotting beside him.

He stopped so abruptly that she was a step ahead of him before she realized he'd paused. When she turned back he was scowling at her.

She ignored his intimidating look. "Could you maybe signal the next time you're going to put on the brakes?" she suggested pleasantly.

"I'm hoping there won't be a next time."

"Gee, you sure know how to make a girl feel wanted."

"I thought I made myself clear yesterday, Ms. Winter. I don't talk to the press. And I did not appreciate the call to my home. I consider that invasion of privacy, not that you reporters know the meaning of that term. But if it happens again, I'll file a complaint. Is that understood?"

She flushed, and something—some odd flash of emotion—darted across her eyes. It was there and gone so quickly, he wondered if he'd imagined it. But he didn't think so. Suddenly the word *cringe* came to mind, and he frowned. How odd—and unlikely. Reporters were a thick-skinned lot. You couldn't hurt their feelings if you tried. Obviously he had misread her reaction.

"Look, Mr. Richards, I'm sorry about the call to your apartment. It seemed like a good idea at the time, but it won't happen again. However, I won't promise to stop calling your office or talking to you here at the courthouse. That's my job." She tilted her chin defiantly on the last words, giving him a good look at her classic oval face, clear, intelligent eyes and determined, nicely shaped lips. His gaze lingered on those lips just a moment too long before he jerked it away, disconcerted by the sudden, unaccountable acceleration of his pulse.

"And my job is to see justice done," he countered a little too sharply as he moved forward once again.

"Why should our two jobs be incompatible? And why do you hate the press so much?" she persisted, struggling to keep pace with his long strides.

They reached the door of the courthouse and he turned to her, his jaw set, his eyes flinty. "They shouldn't be incompatible, Ms. Winter. Justice should be a mutual goal of the press and the law. But the only things TV stations care about are ratings and advertising revenues. If that means sensationalizing a trial at the expense of justice to gain viewers, so be it."

"That's a pretty cynical attitude."

His mouth twisted into a humorless smile. "Let's just call it realistic. How long have you been in this business, Ms. Winter? Two years? Three?"

"Seven."

His eyebrows rose in surprise. She didn't look more than a year or two out of school, but she must be close to thirty, he realized.

"Then you should know that it's hard enough to see justice done when everything works right. It's impossible when the press takes sides."

"I take it you're speaking from personal experience?"

He hesitated, then gave a curt nod. "Five years ago I handled a trial very similar to this one. High-profile figure, well liked. He was charged with rape. He was also the proverbial golden-haired boy. Popular, wealthy, powerful, a churchgoing man with a list of philanthropic endeavors to rival Albert Schweitzer. He had the press eating out of his hand. In fact, the news media did everything it could to discredit and harass the victim. She finally caved in under the pressure. We didn't stand a chance." The bitterness in his voice was unmistakable.

"And..."

At her prompt, Cal turned to her, his rapier-sharp eyes cold as steel. "Two years ago he was charged with rape again. But this time he picked the wrong victim and the wrong place. She was a fighter, and she was determined to make him pay. Not to mention the fact that there were witnesses."

"So in the end, justice was served."

He shrugged. "No thanks to the press. And it depends on what you mean by 'justice.' Yes, he was convicted. But he's still appealing. Worst case, he'll serve a couple of years and be back on the streets. I hardly consider that justice, given the crime."

Amy gave him a quizzical look. "So why did you go into law, if it's so hopeless?"

He gazed at her thoughtfully. "Frankly I've been asking myself that question a lot lately," he replied soberly, surprising her—and himself—with his candor. "I guess I thought I could make a difference. And once in a great while I can. Every now and then, because of my efforts, justice is served and the little guy wins. That's what keeps me going. That's what makes it worthwhile."

His tone once more grew brusque. "Look, Ms. Winter, I can't stop you from covering this trial. But

I can—and do—decline to participate. I'll give you one piece of advice, though. Don't fall into the trap those reporters did in the case I just told you about. Don't be taken in by appearances. Do your homework. Dig. Don't assume that the image Jamie Johnson projects publicly is the real man. You'll do everyone a great service if you treat him as you would any other defendant. And while you're at it, take a look at the issue itself. Too many times people blame liquor for drunk driving instead of focusing on the real problem—irresponsibility. That's a harder issue to tackle. But some thoughtful coverage might go a long way toward placing the blame where it belongs—on the person, not the object. Think about that, Ms. Winter. Try to go for substance over sensationalism.''

She looked at him silently for a moment. ''No matter what I do, I have a feeling nothing will change your mind about the news game,'' she said at last.

Cal's mouth settled into a grim line. ''When somebody dies, it's not a game.''

Amy met his intense gaze steadily. ''I agree. And I appreciate your candor and suggestions. They were very helpful. In fact, I'd welcome any other input or ideas you might have as the trial progresses.''

''Don't hold your breath. As I said, I try to stay as far away from the press as possible.''

''I'll keep trying, you know.''

He shrugged and turned away. ''Suit yourself.''

Amy watched as he disappeared inside, a thoughtful expression on her face. For somebody who didn't talk to the press, he'd certainly given her an earful just now. Which meant he might do so again. And maybe next time he would offer a piece of information that would give her just the edge she was looking for in her coverage.

In the meantime, she intended to take to heart what he had said. While she didn't agree completely with his assessment of the press, he had made some valid points. And he'd given her a couple of ideas for related stories that could round out her coverage when there wasn't much to report on in the trial itself. All in all, it had been a productive morning, she decided. She had some good ideas, and she had a ray of hope—which was probably the last thing Cal Richards had intended to give her, she thought, a wry smile quirking the corners of her mouth.

As she turned to go, she glanced back at the door through which the reticent assistant prosecuting attorney had disappeared. He was an interesting man, she mused. Not to mention good-looking. Too bad they were on opposite sides—in his opinion, at least. Not that it mattered, of course. He wasn't her type anyway. Not even close.

Besides, even if he was, she didn't have time for romance. She had a career to build.

"If looks could kill..."

Cal stopped abruptly outside the jury selection room, the scowl on his face softening as he glanced at his colleague.

"It's not that bad, you know. We'll get this jury. If not in this century, then surely in the next."

This time Cal smiled. Bill Jackson, who could go for the jugular in the courtroom better than anyone

Cal had ever encountered, also had an amazing ability to ease the tension in any situation. It was a pretty unbeatable combination in an attorney, and Cal was glad he was assisting on this trial.

"Believe it or not, I wasn't even thinking about the jury."

"No? Then what put that look on your face?"

"A run-in with the press."

"No kidding! I thought you had them all trained to keep their distance."

"So did I. I think this one's new."

"What's his name?"

"It's a her. Amy Winter."

Bill gave a low whistle, and Cal raised his eyebrows. "You know her?"

"Unfortunately, no. But I've seen her on TV. Man, she's a looker! And you're right. She's only been around a few months. Must be good, though, to get an assignment like this so quickly."

"She's pushy, anyway."

Bill shrugged. "Same thing in the news game."

"Yeah, well, I don't appreciate being called at home."

Bill looked at him in surprise. "How'd she get your unlisted number?"

"Beats me. I didn't ask. I just told her to back off."

"And how did the lady respond to that?"

Cal's scowled returned. "Let's just say I don't think I've seen the last of Amy Winter."

Bill chuckled as he reached over to open the door. "This could be interesting. Two people equally unwilling to bend. You'll have to keep me informed. In the meantime, we'd better get on with the jury selection or there won't even be a trial to write about.''

As Cal followed Bill into the room, he gave one last fleeting thought to Amy Winter. Bill had called her a ''looker,'' and his colleague was right. But that wasn't why she lingered in his memory. He'd met plenty of attractive women, and he'd rarely given them a thought once out of their presence. No, it wasn't her *looks* that intrigued him. It was the *look* that had appeared in her eyes, then quickly vanished, when he'd spoken harshly to her. For the briefest of moments she had seemed somehow...*vulnerable* was the word that came to mind. Yet that seemed so out of character for someone in her profession. Reporters got the cold shoulder all the time. Surely they built up an immunity to it. Why would she be any different?

And she probably wasn't, he told himself brusquely. Most likely he'd imagined the whole thing. Besides, why should he care? Amy Winter was a stranger to him. And a reporter to boot. She was aggressive, ambitious, competitive, single-minded, brash—qualities he didn't particularly admire in either gender. He ought to just forget her and hope she honored his request to back off.

Except he didn't think she would.

And for some strange reason, he didn't think she was going to be so easy to forget.

Chapter Two

Amy took a sip of her drink and glanced around glumly. A charity bachelor auction was the last place she wanted to be on a Saturday night. If her TV station hadn't bought a table and their lead anchorwoman wasn't the MC—making this a politically expedient event to attend—the proverbial wild horses couldn't have dragged her here. Spending an entire evening watching women bid on dates was not exactly her idea of a compelling way to use her precious—and rare—free time.

"Why the long face?"

Amy turned to find one of the younger copywriters from her station at her elbow. She shrugged, groping for the woman's name. Darlene, that was it. "I can think of other places I'd rather be."

"Yeah? Spending an evening mingling with a bunch of hot-looking guys doesn't seem so bad to me. Have you checked out the program?" She waved it in front of Amy's face. "It's got all their pictures and bios."

"No. I'm not planning to bid."

"I wasn't, either, until I got here. But I met several of the auctionees during the cocktail hour and now I've got my eye on Bachelor #12—over there, by the bar." She gazed at him longingly. "Man, a date with that dude would be *worth* a couple hundred bucks! Did you meet anyone interesting?"

Amy shook her head. Actually, she'd only just arrived, putting off her appearance as long as possible. It had been a grueling and frustrating couple of weeks and she was exhausted. Though she'd tried repeatedly to contact Cal Richards—even waylaid him a couple of times enroute to the courthouse—and spent hours in the courtroom after the trial began, he'd hardly spoken to her. Apparently he'd said everything he intended to say at the one encounter when he'd made it clear what he thought of the news media.

Amy sighed. She hadn't given up on finding an angle on this story. But the assistant prosecuting attorney wasn't making it easy, that was for sure. Still, she was due for a break. In fact, she *deserved* one. After all, she'd paid her dues. She'd put in the long hours, sacrificed her personal life, worked the midnight shift in the newsroom, all in the name of career advancement. And she'd accomplished a lot. But not enough. She had her sights set on an anchor slot. And she'd get there, just like Candace Bryce, she vowed, as the celebrity MC stepped to the microphone.

"Ladies, please take your seats so the wait staff can serve dinner—and we can get to the *real* purpose of this evening. You'll have about an hour to enjoy your food and plan your strategy. Bon appétit!''

"Our table's over there," Darlene indicated with a nod, leaving Amy to follow.

Amy knew most of the women from the station either by name or face, although she didn't consider any of them "friends." The broadcast news business was too competitive to foster real friendships. She smiled pleasantly and sat down in the one empty chair, her back to the stage. Obviously her table mates had vied for the seats with the best view, she thought wryly. As far as she was concerned, they could have them. She'd much rather focus on the chocolate mousse promised for dessert than the dessert the other women had in mind.

By the time the mousse was served, Amy was beginning to plan her escape strategy. She'd put in her appearance, been noticed by Candace and stopped on the way to the ladies' room to chat with the station manager. Her duty was done. In another few minutes she could sneak out, head back to her apartment, take her shoes off, put on some mellow jazz, dim the lights and do absolutely nothing for what little remained of the evening. It sounded like heaven!

As Candace stepped once more to the microphone, a buzz of excitement swept over the room and there was a rustling of paper as the women reached for their programs. While the ladies focused on the stage, Amy focused on her dessert.

The first auctionee was introduced to cheers and whistles, and Amy rolled her eyes. How could grown women behave in such a sophomoric way? she wondered in disgust. And *they* complained that *men* acted juvenile! She eyed the exit longingly, but it was too soon to leave. The bidding had barely begun. Resignedly she reached for one of the programs and fished a pen out of her purse. She might as well put the time to good use. In the car this evening, on the way to the dinner, she'd had some ideas about the trial coverage and she wanted to jot them down before they slipped her mind.

As Amy made her notes, she tuned down the surrounding cacophony of sound until it was no more than a background buzz. She'd learned that technique early in her career, when she realized she would often have to compose broadcast copy in the midst of chaos for live feeds. It was a skill that had served her well in the years that followed.

In the one real conversation they'd had, Cal Richards had suggested some angles for her coverage that she hadn't yet explored. She'd also picked up a few ideas since sitting in on the first couple of sessions of the trial. They had all been filed away in her mind for emergency use, just in case she wasn't able to break through his wall of reserve. Up until now, she'd been confident she'd find a way to do that. But her confidence was beginning to slip, she admitted. She'd tried everything she could think of, and the man simply refused to budge. It was time to put some of her emergency plans into action.

Amy ran out of room and turned the page to continue her scribbling. Her name fell on Bachelor #5 just as Candace introduced him.

''Now, ladies, here we have a real coup. One of

Atlanta's most eligible and elusive bachelors, who only agreed to participate because of his interest in Saint Vincent's Boy's Club, which will benefit from this event. He's gorgeous, articulate, charming and *very* available. If I wasn't already married, I'd bid on this one myself. Ladies, please welcome one of Atlanta's finest assistant prosecuting attorneys, Cal Richards.''

Amy practically choked on the sip of coffee she'd just taken as the room erupted into wild applause and more catcalls. She stared at his name and photo in the program, then jerked around to confirm that her nemesis was, indeed, present. Sure enough, there he was, looking incredibly handsome in his tux—and extremely uncomfortable in the glare of the spotlight, judging by the flush on his face and his strained smile. Cal Richards, who shied away from publicity, was allowing himself to be ogled by a roomful of raucous women and auctioned off for charity! It was incredible! It was unbelievable! It was…the chance she'd been waiting for, she realized with a jolt! If she bought a date with him, he'd *have* to talk to her, she reasoned, her mind clicking into high gear. Sure, there was a chance he wouldn't tell her anything of value. But she was pretty good at ferreting out information. It couldn't hurt to try, considering she'd run out of other options.

Amy turned to Darlene. "How much are these guys going for?"

Darlene gave her a distracted glance. "What?"

"How much are these guys going for?" Amy repeated impatiently.

"So…someone caught your eye." Darlene glanced back at the stage and gave Amy a sly smile. "I can't say I blame you. He's a hunk. Even if he wasn't a prosecuting attorney, my defenses would crumble with him in five seconds flat."

The bidding had already started, and Amy needed information—fast. In the interest of time she restrained the impulse to throttle Darlene. "It's for a good cause," she replied with a noncommittal shrug.

Darlene wasn't buying. "Yeah, right."

Amy gave up the pretense of disinterest. "So how much?" she repeated urgently.

"The last guy went for three-fifty."

Amy cringed and glanced back toward the stage. Was it worth the gamble? Cal Richards didn't strike her as the kind of man who would bend. But even if she got one lead, one piece of information that gave her an edge, it would be worth the money. It was almost like an investment in her career, she rationalized.

Amy glanced around. Women were holding up numbers and calling out their bids. She turned back to her table, spotted the large number in the center and reached for it as the bid rose to three hundred.

She waited until the bidding slowed at four-twenty-five.

"Okay, ladies, is that it? Any more bidders? No? All right, then…" Candace raised her gavel. "Going…going…"

Amy took a deep breath, turned her head slightly away just in case Cal Richards could see past the glare of the spotlight, and held up her number. "Four-fifty."

There was a momentary hush, and her heart thumped painfully against her rib cage.

"Four-seventy-five," someone countered.

Amy gulped. "Five hundred."

A murmur swept the room.

"Now, ladies, that's what I call a bid!" Candace said approvingly. "Do I hear five and a quarter?"

Amy stopped breathing. Five hundred was about her limit, especially when the odds of hitting the jackpot were about on a par with winning the lottery.

"No? All right, Bachelor #5 is going, going, gone, to table thirty-two and one very lucky lady."

As enthusiastic applause swept the room and her table mates congratulated her, Amy hoped Candace was right. Because she could use a little luck about now.

"Cal, there's a woman on the phone who says she won you in an auction. Is she a nut, or is there something you haven't told me?"

Cal closed his eyes and felt the beginning of a headache prick at his temples. He hadn't mentioned the auction to anyone in his office, especially not Cynthia. She was a great friend and legal assistant, but ever since she'd walked down the aisle a year ago, she'd made it her personal goal in life to watch him do the same. And she was nothing if not tenacious. "She's not a nut, Cynthia, and yes, there's something I haven't told you."

As the silence lengthened, he could feel her growing impatience over the line.

"So are you going to come clean of your own free will or do I have to drag it out of you?" she finally demanded.

A bemused smile tipped up the corners of his mouth. "Have you ever thought about going into police work, Cyn? You'd be great at the third degree."

"Hah-hah. Spill it, Richards."

He sighed. There was no way around it. He and Cynthia had been co-workers and friends a long time, and she wouldn't rest until she had the whole story. "I agreed to be one of the bachelors auctioned off at a charity dinner last Friday. A good chunk of the money goes to Saint Vincent's, so I couldn't say no."

"No kidding! Mr. Particular, who finds fault with everyone I suggest as a potential date, is actually going to go out with some strange woman?"

"I certainly hope she's not strange."

"Very funny. So do you want to talk to her or not?"

Cal sighed again. No, he didn't. But he'd have to face this sooner or later, and he might as well get it over with. "Yeah, I guess so."

"Do try to restrain your eagerness," Cynthia said dryly. "Remember, this woman paid good money for you. You could at least show a little enthusiasm. How much, by the way?"

"Five hundred."

She gave a low whistle. "All I can say is, you better make this date something to remember. I'll put her through."

"Wait! Did she give you her name?"

"No. Don't you have it?" Cynthia asked in surprise.

"I cut out early that night. She hadn't gone back to pay yet. They said she'd be in touch with me."

"Well, it's payoff time now. Have fun, lover boy."

Cal grimaced and took a deep breath. This was the most awkward thing he'd ever done, even if it was for a good cause. He just hoped the woman could at least carry on a decent conversation, or it would be one very long evening.

He heard the call go through and, remembering Cynthia's comment about how much money the bidder had paid, forced a pleasant note into his voice. "Cal Richards speaking."

"Mr. Richards, I believe we have a date."

He frowned. The voice was oddly—and unsettlingly—familiar, and a wave of uneasiness swept over him.

"Yes, I think we do," he replied warily. "I'm sorry, I didn't get your name the night of the dinner, although I have a feeling we've met."

"Yes, we have. This is Amy Winter."

Amy Winter? The *reporter?* Impossible! Fate wouldn't be that unkind, not after he'd endured being auctioned off in front of hundreds of women, let himself be humiliated for charity. It couldn't be her!

"Mr. Richards, are you still there?"

It was her, all right, he realized with a sinking feeling. Now that she'd identified herself, he recognized that distinctive, slightly husky voice. His headache suddenly took a turn for the worst, and he closed his eyes. "Yes, I'm here. Look, Ms. Winter, is this a joke?"

"Hardly. I paid good money for this date. And I have the receipt to prove it."

"But why in the world...?" His voice trailed off as her strategy suddenly became clear. He wouldn't talk to her in a business setting, so she figured he'd have to in a social situation. A muscle in his jaw clenched, and his headache ratcheted up another notch. "It won't work, you know," he said coldly.

"What?"

"Don't play innocent with me, Ms. Winter. You're still trying to get me to talk about the trial. Well, forget it. You wasted five hundred dollars."

"It went to a good cause. Besides, how do you know I didn't bid on you because I really wanted a date?"

"Ms. Winter, anyone who looks like you doesn't need to buy dates at an auction. Let's stop playing games. You bought a date, I'll give you a date. And that's all I'll give you. How about dinner Friday night?"

"How about sooner?"

"Sorry, that's the best I can do."

"Okay. Just name the time and place."

"I'll pick you up. That was part of the deal."

"Don't put yourself out."

Cal frowned. She sounded miffed. And she had a right to, he conceded guiltily. As Cynthia had said, she'd paid good money for their date, whatever her motivation. He took a deep breath and forced a more pleasant tone into his voice. "I'll be happy to pick you up. Just give me your address."

She hesitated, and for a moment he thought she was going to refuse. But in the end she relented and they settled on a time.

"I'll see you Friday, Mr. Richards. It should be interesting."

That wasn't exactly the word he would have chosen, he thought grimly as he hung up the phone, reached for his coffee and shook out two aspirin from the bottle he kept in his desk drawer. On second thought, he made it three. Amy Winter was definitely a three-aspirin headache.

As Amy replaced the receiver, she realized her hand was shaking. The strain of keeping up a breezy front with the recalcitrant assistant prosecuting attorney had clearly taken a toll. She'd always been outspoken and assertive, but "pushy" wasn't her style. Which was unfortunate, given the career she'd chosen. Though she'd learned to be brash, she hadn't yet learned to like it. The in-your-face approach just wasn't her. But it *was* part of the job, and she figured in time it would get easier. The only problem was, she'd been telling herself that for years now.

Amy took a sip of her herbal tea and gave herself a few minutes to calm down. Cal Richards didn't like her, and though she knew she shouldn't let that bother her, it did. She liked to be liked. But she'd chosen the wrong business for that, she reminded herself wryly. Investigative reporters didn't usually win popularity contests. Acrimony went with the territory.

For a fleeting moment Amy wondered if she might have been happier using her reporting skills in some other way. But she ruthlessly stifled that unsettling thought almost as quickly as it arose. It was way too late for second-guessing. She'd invested too much of her life and energy building this particular future to question it now. She'd very deliberately set her sights on a career as an anchorwoman, and she knew exactly why.

First, she liked the glamour. She enjoyed being in the spotlight, relished her pseudocelebrity status.

Second, she liked the big-city lifestyle. Unlike her sister, Kate, who had actually enjoyed small-town farm life, Amy had always dreamed of the bright lights and the excitement of the city. If the lights were more garish than dazzling up close, well, that was more a reflection of the nature of her work—which often took her to seedy areas—than of the actual city, she assured herself.

Third, she liked the money. Or at least the freedom it gave her. The freedom to travel to the Caribbean on exotic vacations, the freedom to live in an upscale town house, the freedom to walk into any store in Atlanta and buy whatever designer outfit she chose without having to give up something else to do so. Money had always been tight on the farm. Her parents had done their best, but she had vowed to put the days of homemade prom dresses and hand-me-downs far behind her.

Fourth, she liked feature reporting, especially human-interest stories that uplifted and inspired and made people feel optimistic about the goodness of the human race. True, those rarely came her way. Someday, though, when she made her mark, she would be able to pick and choose her assignments, decide when and if she wanted to come out from behind the anchor desk. But that was still a long way down the road. In the meantime, she did what she was told and worked hard to get the best possible story. Including bidding on a date with a man who clearly disliked her.

Amy sighed and took another sip of tea, trying to find something positive in the situation. She thought back over their conversation and suddenly recalled Cal's comment about her not needing to buy a date. So he thought she was attractive, she mused. It wasn't much, she acknowledged, but it was a start.

"Hi, Gram. How's everything at home?"

"Cal? My, it's good to hear your voice! We're both fine. Jack, it's Cal," she called, her voice muffled as she apparently turned her head.

Cal smiled and leaned back, resting his head against the cushion of the overstuffed chair as he crossed an ankle over his knee. Just hearing the voices from home made him feel better.

"Your dad'll be right here, son. How's life in Atlanta?"

"Okay."

"Hmph. I've heard more enthusiasm from old Sam Pritchard."

Cal smiled again. Sam Pritchard was legendary in the mountains for his blasé reaction to life. As usual, his grandmother had tuned right in to Cal's mood.

Probably because she was one of the few people who knew of his growing dissatisfaction with city life.

"Sorry, Gram." He modified his tone. "I can't complain. The job is demanding and stressful, but it's worthwhile work, and I've been blessed in a lot of ways."

"Are you taking any time for fun?"

Cal pondered that question. Fun? The only time he really had any fun was when he went home, and that wasn't often enough. When he was in the city, he was too busy for much socializing. His job ate up an inordinate amount of his time, and most of the little that remained he spent at Saint Vincent's.

"I get out once in a while," he hedged.

"You need to take some time for yourself, son," the older woman persisted, the worry evident in her voice. "A body needs more in life than work and responsibilities. You meet any nice women lately?"

For some reason, his social life—or lack thereof—had become a hot topic over the past year. His grandmother seemed to think that if he got married and had a family, many of his doubts and issues would be resolved. Frankly, he thought a romantic entanglement would just complicate matters. He needed to get his life in order, make some decisions about his future, before he got involved in a relationship. That was only fair to the woman. And it was that sense of fairness, not lack of interest, that kept him from serious dating. In fact, in the past couple of years he'd begun to long for the very things his grandmother was suggesting, had become increasingly aware of an emotional vacuum in his life. He'd lain awake more nights than he cared to admit yearning for warmth, for a caring touch, for someone who would listen to the secrets of his heart and share hers with him. He *wanted* to fall in love. It was just that now was not the time.

"Cal?" his grandmother prompted. "It wasn't a hard question. 'Course, if it's none of my business, that's okay."

"Actually, I have a date Friday night," he offered, to appease her.

"Well! Now that's fine."

He could hear the surprise in her voice, could tell she was pleased, and he felt a twinge of guilt. He should explain the situation. After all, it wasn't a real date.

"It's no big deal, Gram. Just dinner."

"Everything has to start somewhere. Where did you meet her?" she asked eagerly.

He felt himself getting in deeper. "At the courthouse. But Gram, she…"

"Is she a lawyer, too?"

"No. She works in TV. Actually, that's how…"

"My! That sounds interesting. What's her—oh, your dad's ready to talk to you. We'll catch up some more later. You call us again over the weekend, okay?"

Cal sighed as the phone was passed on. He'd certainly handled that well, he berated himself. Now his grandmother would get her hopes up, jump to all sorts of wrong conclusions. But he'd be better prepared when he called the next time. He'd use the old "we just didn't click" routine, and that would be the end of that.

"Cal? How are you, son?"

Cal settled deeper into the chair. "Hi, Dad. Fine. How's everything there?"

"Same as always. Quiet. Things don't change much in the mountains, you know. But tell me about you. I know there's a lot more going on in Atlanta than there is here."

Cal relayed some recent events that he knew his father would enjoy hearing about—the black-tie dinner, though he made no mention of the auction part of the evening, a meeting he'd had with the mayor earlier in the week, the publicity the Jamie Johnson trial was receiving. As usual, his father ate it up.

"My, son! You sure do lead an exciting life. But you deserve all your success. You worked hard for it. And I'm proud of you. I was just telling Mike Thomas about the governor's commission you were appointed to. He was real impressed."

Cal felt the old familiar knot begin to form in his gut. His father was a kind, gentle, decent man who'd never had a break in his entire life. He'd spent his youth and middle age barely scraping by, handicapped by limited education and limited opportunity as he struggled to support a son and an ailing wife. He'd worked with his hands all his life, accepting that as his lot but dreaming of better things for Cal. Now he was living Cal's success vicariously. If his son returned to the mountains, in whatever capacity, the older man would be sorely disappointed, Cal knew. But there had to be a line somewhere between responsibility to his father and to himself. He just wasn't sure where it was.

Up until now he'd done everything that was expected of him—by others and by himself. He gave his job one hundred percent, and did his best to make a contribution to society. He'd provided well for Gram and his dad. They'd refused his offer to move to Atlanta, both reluctant to leave the only home they'd ever known, but he made sure they lived comfortably, that neither had to work anymore. By choice, Gram still put in a great deal of time at the craft co-op she'd founded. His father, however, who had always disliked working the land, had walked away from his job without a second look, content to spend his time helping out at the church or reading, a pastime he'd had little opportunity to indulge in most of his life. *They* were both happy. Unfortunately, the vague discontent that had been nagging him for years had intensified dramatically in the last few months, leaving *him* restless and searching.

"You coming home to visit soon, son?" His father interrupted his thoughts.

"I hope so, Dad." The sudden weariness in his voice reflected the burden of decision he was struggling with, and he tried for a more upbeat tone. "It's hard to get away, though. Things are pretty busy."

"I understand. You have an important job. I'm sure they need you there. But your room is always waiting, anytime you can get away. You'll come up sometime later in the spring, won't you?"

"Of course. Have I ever missed spring in the mountains?"

The older man chuckled. "Can't say you have. One thing about you, son. You're reliable. We can always count on you."

The knot in Cal's gut tightened. "I'm not perfect, Dad."

"Maybe not. But I sure wouldn't trade you in. You take care, now."

"All right, Dad. Tell Gram I said goodbye."

Cal replaced the receiver and wearily let his head drop back against the chair. He needed to make some decisions, and he needed to make them soon. There were rumors that he was being considered for a promotion to the coveted position of prosecuting attorney. He should be happy. It was what he was supposed to have been working toward all these years. Instead, it just made him feel more pressured, more trapped. If he was going to make a change, this was the time, before he got so deeply entrenched in his urban career and lifestyle that he couldn't get out.

Cal closed his eyes. He wanted to go back to the mountains, back to the place where he felt more in touch with nature, with himself and with his God. Cal hadn't let his spiritual life slip since coming to the city. It was too important to him to neglect. But it was harder here to retain a sense of balance, to stay focused on the really important things in life. There were too many distractions, too many demands, too much emphasis on materialism, power, prestige and "getting ahead."

Cal's priorities had always been different. Position and money meant nothing to him personally. Their only value, as far as he could see, was that they gave him the means to help others who were less fortunate. In his job, he did his best to see justice served, which helped humanity in general. That, in turn, provided a good income, which allowed him to make life better for Gram and his father. And he was able to contribute both time and dollars to the causes he believed in, such as Saint Vincent's. So plenty of good had come from his career choice. Was he being selfish to consider changing the status quo?

Cal rose, walked restlessly over to the window and stared pensively out at the city lights. In his heart, he wanted to go home, back to the mountains where he could spend his days free of the confines of concrete and steel and glass. There was a part of him deep inside that had always yearned to share the beauty of nature with others hungry for nourishment for their souls. Though he had no specific plans for it, he'd completed a degree in forestry last year by going to night school. It was just something he'd wanted to do, and he'd shared the accomplishment with very few. Even Gram didn't know.

Cal sighed. He knew that few people would understand his feelings about the mountains. Certainly no one in the city, and very few at home. Gram did. But not his father. And the last thing he wanted to do was disappoint the man who had sacrificed so much for him. As his father saw it, Cal was his one success in life. If Cal scaled down his lifestyle, gave up his high-profile job and moved back home, his father would feel that all his efforts had been for nothing, that he was a failure after all. And Cal didn't know if he could do that to the man who had given him life and love so abundantly. Nor was he sure he should walk away from his present job, knowing he was good at it and that he did, sometimes, make a difference.

Cal jammed his fists into his pockets and looked up at the sky, trying to discern the stars that shone so brightly in the mountains but here were dimmed by the glare of city lights.

Lord, I need Your guidance, he prayed. *I want to do the right thing, but I need direction. I need to know Your will. You know I want to go home, that my heart is most at peace in the mountains. But maybe my dad's needs and my work here are more important. Please help me make the decision that best serves You. And, Lord—please do it soon. Because I feel like a man in limbo. I'm torn between two worlds, and I don't think I can give my best to either until this issue is resolved.*

Chapter Three

Amy took one last look in the mirror, nervously brushed a stray strand of hair back into place and glanced at her watch. Cal Richards was late.

For a moment she wondered if he'd stood her up, then quickly dismissed her doubt. There might be many things she didn't like about the assistant prosecuting attorney, but somehow she sensed he was a man of honor who played by the rules and kept his promises. If he was late, there was a reason.

Amy had no idea where they were going for dinner, so she'd chosen a middle-of-the-road outfit—nice enough for a dressy place, but not too dressy for a casual restaurant. She looked at herself critically. Since the only pleasant thing Cal Richards had ever said to her related to her appearance, she'd taken pains to look especially nice tonight. Her fashionably short, slim black skirt and two-inch heels enhanced the line of her legs, and the jade-green, jewel-neckline jacquard silk blouse softly hugged her curves and shimmered in the light. A wide, black leather belt emphasized her small waist, and a clunky hammered gold necklace and matching earrings added an elegant touch. She'd softened her usual sleek, businesslike hairstyle by blow-drying her fine hair into gentle waves that fluffed around her shoulders, and she'd added a touch of eye shadow that brought out the green of her eyes.

Amy studied her image for another moment, then gave a satisfied nod. This was definitely the right look, she decided. She could be any young woman going out on a Friday-night date. The fact that there was an ulterior motive—well, if she was lucky, Cal Richards would quickly forget all about that.

The doorbell rang and Amy's pulse kicked into high gear. She forced herself to take a couple of deep, steadying breaths, squared her shoulders, plastered an artificial smile on her face and then walked purposefully toward the door, determined to give this evening her best shot. As she reached for the knob, the image of a boxing match, complete with a gong followed by the voice of an announcer saying "Round one," suddenly flashed through her mind. An appropriate analogy, she reflected, her lips quirking wryly. Then, with her adrenaline pumping for the battle of wits ahead, she opened the door.

The sight that greeted her instantly wiped the smile off her face. It appeared Cal Richards had already fought round one—and lost. His tie was askew, his hair was mussed and he was holding a bloody handkerchief to his nose and sporting a rapidly blackening eye.

She stared at him speechlessly for several seconds before she found her voice. "Good heavens, what happened?" she finally sputtered, her face a mask of shock.

"Where's your phone?"

"What?"

"Your phone. I need to report a mugging."

Her eyes widened. "You're kidding!"

He glared at her, his voice muffled behind the handkerchief. "Do I look like I'm kidding?"

"No. I mean...I can't believe this! Look, come in. Sit down. Are you all right?" She took his arm and guided him toward the couch, pushing the door shut with her foot. Once he was seated she scurried for the portable phone and handed it to him. "I'll get some ice. And a towel."

"Don't bother."

She ignored him and headed toward the kitchen. By the time she returned, the phone was lying on the coffee table and he was trying vainly to staunch the flow of blood with his very inadequate handkerchief. She thrust the towel into his hand.

"Here. Use this. And tilt your head back. Then put this on your eye." She placed the ice bag in his other hand.

"Has anyone ever told you you're bossy?" he grumbled, wincing as he gingerly settled the ice bag against his bruised skin.

She grinned. "I think my sister might have said that a few times through the years."

"Well, she was right. Listen, the police will be here in a few minutes. I'm sorry to put you in the middle of this."

"Do you want to tell me what happened?"

"Two thugs jumped me in the parking lot. I didn't even see them coming," he said in disgust. "I'm usually more alert than that." And he would have been tonight, too, if he hadn't been so preoccupied with this obligatory date, he thought ruefully.

Amy frowned and sank into the nearest chair. "I've never heard of anything like that happening here before."

"There's always a first time. No place is really safe, Ms. Winter. You ought to know that. You cover the crime beat."

She sighed. "Look, can we move past the 'Mr.' and 'Ms.' business? It's starting to seem kind of silly."

Even with only one good eye, his piercing gaze was intimidating, and she shifted uncomfortably. But instead of responding, he suddenly closed his eyes and leaned wearily back against the couch.

Amy frowned. He looked pale. Maybe he was hurt worse than he was letting on, she thought worriedly as a wave of panic swept over her.

"Look, Mr. Richards, are you sure you don't need an ambulance or something?" She rose and hovered over him nervously.

He opened his good eye and she thought she saw a glimmer of amusement in its depths. "Just make it Cal. And no, I'll be okay. But thanks."

The doorbell rang, and with one last worried glance at him, she hurried to answer it.

For the next few minutes she stayed in the background while the officer and Cal spoke. They obviously knew each other, and their mutual respect was evident. Cal described the two young men as best he could, told the officer they'd only been interested in the hundred dollars in his money clip and roughing him up a bit, and once more declined medical assistance.

"I've been taken care of," he said, directing a brief smile toward Amy.

"Okay, then." The officer stood and closed his notebook. "I'm awfully sorry about this, Cal."

"It's not your fault, Mitch. You guys do the best you can. You can't be everywhere at once."

There was a warmth in Cal's voice that Amy had never heard before, and she looked at him curiously. Up until now, she'd only seen two sides of him—the incisive prosecuting attorney at work in the courtroom, and the reticent, abrupt, potential news source who held her profession, and as a result, her, in low esteem. This human side, this warmth, was new. And quite refreshing. Not to mention appealing, she realized with a jolt.

"We haven't had much trouble in this area before." The officer frowned and sent a troubled look toward Amy. "Have you heard or seen anything suspicious recently, ma'am?"

"No. Never. But I've only lived here six months."

Mitch stared at her for a moment. "Aren't you on TV? One of the news shows?"

"Yes."

"This would have to happen on my beat," he said in dismay. "Listen, you're not going to…"

"No!" Cal and Amy answered in unison, and with equal vehemence. He sent her an amused look and she flushed.

"There's more important news to report than a mugging," Amy said with a shrug.

"Yeah." Mitch frowned and turned his attention back to Cal. "This was probably just a freak incident. Still, we'll beef up patrols in this area for a while. And if we get any leads on those two, we'll let you know."

"Thanks."

Amy let the officer out, then returned to the living room. Cal was standing now, the ice pack still clamped against his eye, but his nose had stopped bleeding. "Could I use your bathroom? I'd like to clean up a little."

"Sure. Right down the hall."

She watched him disappear, then sank onto the sleek, modular couch. She'd speculated all week about how this evening would play out, but never in a million years would she have dreamed up this scenario!

Cal was gone a long time, and when he returned the only lingering physical evidence of the mugging was the black eye. Aside from that, he looked great, she realized, getting past his face for the first time all evening. His dark gray suit sat well on his broad shoulders, and she figured he must put in time at a gym to maintain such a trim, athletic appearance. Despite the trauma of the past hour, his white shirt still looked crisp, and his elegant red-and-navy-striped tie was now ramrod straight. He'd restored order to his thick, dark brown hair, as well, and for once his brown eyes seemed friendly rather than adversarial.

"Feeling better?" she asked.

"Much. I rinsed out the towel. It should be okay after it's washed, but I'll be happy to replace it if you prefer."

Amy waved his suggestion aside. "Don't even think about it. I'm just sorry about all this." She sighed and leaned back. "Well, so much for our date."

He weighed the ice pack in his hand and raised his brows quizzically. "Are you calling it off?"

She looked at him in surprise. "Aren't you? I mean, you were just mugged! You can't possibly feel like going out."

He shrugged. "I'll admit those two thugs hurt my pride. And my pocketbook. But not my appetite. And I still have my credit cards. I'm willing to give it a shot, as long as you don't mind being seen with a guy who has a shiner. Besides, this way I can get all the unpleasantness out of the way in one night—a mugging and this date." His teasing tone and crooked grin softened his words.

Amy stared at him. He was actually smiling at her! Genuinely smiling! And suddenly her pulse did the oddest thing. It started to race. Not the way it did when she was nervous about confronting a hostile source for a story. No, this was altogether different. This was almost a pleasant sensation. And why on

earth had a thrilling little tingle just run up her spine?
Good heavens, if she didn't know better, she'd think
she was attracted to the man! Which was ridiculous.
After all, this wasn't even a real date. It was a strategy. And she would do well to remember that, she
admonished herself.

Amy swallowed and tried for a flippant tone. "Putting my date on par with a mugging isn't the most
flattering comparison I've ever heard."

He smiled again. "You must admit there is a sim-
ilarity. The muggers wanted money, you want information. But I guarantee they were more successful
than you'll be."

"Maybe I should resort to strong-arming, like they
did," she replied pertly, getting into the teasing spirit.

He eyed her speculatively, the quick sweep of his
gaze lingering just a bit too long on her shapely,
crossed legs. "Unless you're a black belt, I don't
think that will work. Or maybe you're referring to
something besides physical force," he countered with
a lazy smile.

Amy stared at him. The man was actually flirting
with her! The buttoned-up, stuffed-shirt, play-by-the-
rules assistant prosecuting attorney was letting his
hair down! The transformation in his demeanor was
amazing! Apparently he had a sense of humor after
all.

Or did he? she wondered, her eyes suddenly growing troubled. Maybe he *wasn't* teasing. Maybe he was
hinting that he might be willing to answer her questions if she cooperated in other ways. He *had* made
it clear that he thought she was attractive. He hadn't

struck her as the type to even think along those lines, but, after all, she hardly knew him. And it wouldn't be the first time someone had suggested such a thing. She just hadn't expected it from him, she admitted, oddly disappointed. He seemed somehow to radiate integrity and honor and...well, goodness, corny as that might sound.

Amy hoped her first impression was right, that his last remark had just been innocent flirting, but in case she was wrong, she needed to clarify the parameters of this date right now. She rose, tilted her chin up and gazed at him levelly.

"Look, Mr. Richards, don't get the wrong idea. I—"

"I thought we were past the 'Mr.' stage."

"Maybe. Maybe not. I don't know what you're thinking right now, and I might be jumping to conclusions, but let me make something very clear. I want to find a way to make my coverage on the Jamie Johnson story stand out. I want that very much. Enough to go to some pretty extreme lengths, including spending five hundred dollars for a date with a man who dislikes me on the slim chance that I might get some piece of information I can use. But I don't intend to make a...personal...investment in this story. That's not my style. It never has been, and it never will be."

Now it was Cal's turn to stare. Good heavens, did she really think he was insinuating that for the right "personal investment," as she put it, he might be willing to offer her a few crumbs of information? What kind of man did she think he was? he thought indignantly. He opened his mouth to set her straight, then suddenly recalled some advice Gram had once offered, which had always held him in good stead: Think before you speak. And put yourself in the other person's shoes before jumping to conclusions.

He stifled his sharp retort and instead took a moment to study the woman across from him, looking for the first time past her superficial beauty. There was spirit in her deep green eyes, and intelligence and sensitivity, he realized. Her posture was defiant, but the subtle quiver in her hand as she reached up to brush a stray strand of hair back from her face was more revealing. To the world she might appear brash and assertive and so ambitious that she was willing to push the bounds of ethics for the sake of a scoop, but suddenly he knew better. Amy Winter had principle. And character. Yes, she wanted success. But not at any price.

He admired her for that, admired her for setting clear boundaries and taking a stand. After all, she really didn't know him, he reminded himself, and the crime beat was filled with seedy characters. With her looks, she'd probably been propositioned more times than she could remember as a trade-off for information. Once more he felt a surge of anger. Not *at* her this time, but *for* her. She'd obviously been subjected to offensive behavior and suggestions often enough to make her suspect his motives.

Instinctively he reached out to touch her arm, but at her startled jerk, he withdrew his hand immediately. He could feel her tension quivering almost palpably in the room. She was like a young colt, he realized. Skittish and suddenly unsure and ready to bolt at the slightest provocation. It was not the behavior he'd expected from the sophisticated, glib, always-in-control newswoman he'd encountered up until now.

"Look, let's sit down for a minute, okay?" he suggested gently.

She eyed him warily, trying to read the expression in his eyes. The man was like a chameleon, changing from moment to moment. She could deal with the difficult, evasive assistant prosecuting attorney. She was used to that type. She could also deal with men who thought they could barter for favors. Unfortunately, she'd had experience with that type, too. But the way Cal Richards was looking at her now—with compassion and concern and a disconcerting insight—threw her off balance. And for a woman who liked to be in control, that was *not* a pleasant sensation. After all, *she* might know that confrontation made her uncomfortable, but she'd always done a good job hiding that from the world. Until now. For some reason, she had a feeling Cal had picked up on it. And that was downright scary. A "danger" signal flashed in her mind, and somehow she sensed that it would be a lot safer if he left right now, if they forgot about this date and—

"Please."

The single word, quietly spoken, and the warmth in his eyes, melted her resistance. Even though she had a feeling she was making a mistake, she did as he asked and gingerly sat on the couch, folding her hands tightly in her lap. He sat beside her, keeping a modest distance between them.

"I think we need to clear the air here," he said, his gaze locked on hers. "I was only teasing a few minutes ago. For the record, I do not indulge in, nor condone, physical affection except in the context of a committed relationship. It seems that might be one of the few things you and I agree on. Besides keeping my mugging out of the news, that is."

He smiled then, his eyes reassuring and warm, and Amy looked down, twisting her hands in her lap, feeling like an idiot for overreacting. There was no way she could doubt his sincerity, and a flush of embarrassment rose to her cheeks. Drawing a deep breath, she forced herself to meet his gaze.

"I'm sorry I jumped to conclusions," she said quietly.

"I have a feeling you had reason to."

She conceded the point with a nod. "I don't always meet the most ethical people in my work."

"I can imagine."

She looked down again. "Listen, why don't you just go home and get some rest? You've been through enough tonight. Just forget about the date, okay?"

Cal frowned and studied her profile: smooth forehead, finely shaped nose, firm chin, the slender sweep of her neck. At the moment she looked more like a fragile and vulnerable woman than a brash reporter. An unexpected surge of protectiveness swept over him, and his frown deepened. Now what was *that* all about? He didn't even *like* Amy Winter! And she'd just let him off the hook, released him from the obligation to go on the date he'd been dreading. This was his chance to make a quick exit. Except, strangely enough, he suddenly didn't want to leave.

When the silence lengthened, Amy glanced up cautiously and tried to smile. "Are you still here? I thought you'd be out the door in three seconds after that reprieve."

So had he. Why was he still sitting here? For a man who spent his days finding answers to difficult questions, this one left him stumped. Maybe it was simply his sense of fairness, he rationalized. After all, she'd paid good money for this evening, and he owed her dinner. That was certainly the easy answer—even if he had the uncomfortable feeling it wasn't the *right* one. But now was not the time to analyze his motivation for wanting to stay. He could think about that later. In fact, he *would* think about it later—whether he wanted to or not, he realized ruefully. And he had a feeling that the answer was going to be a whole lot more complicated than simple fairness. Still, it was a good enough response to Amy's question.

"I owe you dinner. And I pay my debts."

She hesitated. Then, with a little shrug, she capitulated. "We could at least make it another night, if you'd prefer."

"Like I said, as long as you don't mind having an escort who attracts attention, I'm game."

With or without the black eye, Cal Richards would attract attention, Amy thought. Tall, distinguished, handsome—he'd turn women's heads in any room he entered. If he thought the black eye was the only reason he'd be noticed, he was either slow or totally without vanity. And she knew it wasn't the former. The fact that it must be the latter was refreshing. In her world, appearance—for both men and women—was at least as important as skill and often received far more attention. To discover someone who seemed totally unaware of his appeal was a rare—and pleasant—occurrence.

"I'm used to attention," she hedged.

"I'm sure you are. Even Mitch recognized you. I imagine that gets old."

She shrugged. "Not yet. It's still kind of fun, most of the time."

Cal shook his head. "Well, to each his own. Personally I prefer anonymity."

"Then maybe we *should* cancel tonight. Because between the two of us, I guarantee we're going to attract attention."

He frowned. "Well, I have an idea, although it's not much of a date for five hundred dollars," he said slowly.

"What?"

"Let's have dinner here."

She stared at him. "Are you serious?"

"Absolutely."

Amy hesitated, then shrugged. "Okay." She took a quick mental inventory of her freezer. "I think I have a couple of frozen microwave dinners. And I might have a—"

"Whoa!" He held up his hands. "I wasn't asking you to supply the food."

She frowned. "Then what did you have in mind? Pizza?"

He grinned. "Hardly. Will you trust me on this?"

She shrugged. "Why not? Nothing else tonight has turned out the way I expected."

"Look at the bright side. The evening has to get better, because it can't get any worse."

Amy had to admit that he was being an awfully good sport about the whole thing, and she smiled in return. "Too true."

"I'll just need to use your phone again."

"Okay. I'll set the table."

"We'll salvage this evening yet," he promised with an engaging grin as he reached for the phone.

As Amy got out plates and silverware, she glanced once or twice toward Cal. He was mostly turned away from her, but she caught a glimpse of his strong profile now and then. He wasn't exactly handsome in the classic sense, but there was something about his face, some compelling quality—call it "character" for lack of a better term—that touched her. It was odd, really. In an evening full of surprises, this was the most surprising of all—the discovery that she was actually starting to *like* Cal Richards. It didn't make any sense, of course. She was still convinced they were polar opposites in many ways, not to mention at odds professionally. Nevertheless she had a strange feeling that somewhere deep inside, at some core level, they were more alike than either had suspected. It was an intriguing, unsettling and surprising thought.

But the surprises for the evening weren't over yet, it seemed. When she returned to the living room, Cal had put on one of her favorite jazz CDs.

"I like your taste in music," he commented.

"Thanks."

"Dinner will be here shortly."

"Can I ask what we're having?"

He grinned. "I think I'll surprise you."

She tilted her head, a small smile lifting her lips. "I like surprises."

"Really? I'll have to remember that."

She started to say "Why?" then caught herself. It was just a meaningless remark. After tonight, the only time their paths would cross would be in the courtroom, she reminded herself, surprised at the sudden slump in her spirits. She forced herself to focus on the present, reminding herself she had a job to do tonight. That was what this evening was all about after all. With an effort she smiled. "Would you like something to drink?"

"That would be great."

"Would you like a soft drink, or something stronger?"

"Do you have any wine?"

Amy bit her lip. She was pretty sure she had some wine left from a gathering she'd had at Christmastime. "I think so."

"It's not something I indulge in often, but I could use a glass tonight."

Amy returned to the kitchen and rummaged around in the refrigerator, triumphantly withdrawing a bottle of merlot. She had just enough for two glasses, which she carried back to the living room, handing one to Cal.

He waited until she was seated, then lifted his glass. "May the rest of the evening be better," he said.

She raised her glass. "I'll second that."

Amy wasn't sure if it was the toast or the wine or just the fact that they both seemed to let their guard down, but from that moment on, the evening took a decided turn for the better.

By the time they'd finished their wine, dinner arrived, and it was like no "carryout" Amy had ever seen. It came via courier—two gourmet dinners from one of the city's finest restaurants, on china plates inside domed food warmers, complete with salad and a chocolate dessert to die for.

Amy could only stare in awe as Cal arranged the food on the table, shaking her head in wonder the whole time. "Well, if you can't go to the restaurant, bring the restaurant to you," she murmured finally. "I'm impressed. You must have good connections to get this kind of treatment. I didn't think 'carryout' was even in their vocabulary."

Cal shrugged. "The owner and I go way back. Trust me. I'll owe him for this," he said over his shoulder with a grin. Then he stepped back and surveyed the table. "Now, all we need is a little candlelight, and we can pretend we're actually at the restaurant."

"That I can supply."

As they leisurely made their way through the dinner, Amy realized that she was truly enjoying herself. Cal was a good conversationalist, moving with ease from topic to topic, displaying an impressive knowledge and insight on everything from world events to Broadway musicals. The more they talked, the more she realized how much they had in common. Their tastes in art and music were similar, and they were surprisingly in sync politically. It wasn't until they started talking about more personal things, especially their careers, that their differences emerged.

"So tell me why you went into broadcast news," he said as they sipped their coffee and dug into the rich dessert.

Amy cupped her chin in her hand. "For the glamour. And the excitement. Not to mention it pays well," she said with a grin.

"Is money that important?"

"It is when you don't have it."

"So I take it you don't come from a wealthy background."

She made a face. "Hardly. I grew up on a farm in Ohio. We weren't poor, but there was never any money to spare. It never bothered my sister, Kate. She was perfectly content with that life and had no desire to leave the farm. I, on the other hand, was drawn to the lights of the big city. I figured there was more to life than cows and plows, and I was determined to find it."

"Have you?"

She looked surprised. "Sure. I mean, this—" her arm swept the room, with its panoramic view of the city lights "—is what I've always wanted."

"And you've never looked back? Never questioned your decision?"

Amy shifted uncomfortably under his suddenly intense gaze. Funny he should ask that, when she'd done that very thing not long ago. But as she'd told herself then, it was too late for second thoughts. And anyway, she *did* like her life and her job.

"Not really. Sure, there are some parts of my job that I don't particularly care for. But someday, if I play my cards right, I'll snag an anchor slot and have the freedom to pick and choose the kind of stories I cover."

"Such as?"

"Human-interest pieces. Stories about ordinary people who do extraordinary things. Feature reporting, more in-depth than what I do now, where you have the time to do stories that leave people uplifted and inspired. I get to do a bit of that now, but not nearly enough. It's really satisfying to shine the light on good, decent people instead of the dregs of humanity who usually dominate the news. There *are* good people out there, and I like to find ways to give them their moment in the spotlight. I think it would also help young people to see that nice guys don't always finish last."

Amy had gotten more and more passionate as she spoke, and Cal's attentive—and approving—gaze, as well as the sudden warmth in his eyes, brought a flush to her cheeks. She didn't usually get so carried away, nor did she typically reveal so much about her personal feelings. She had no idea why she'd done so tonight. She *did* know it was time to shift the focus. "So now you know all the reasons why I left the farm and never looked back," she finished lightly. "And how about you? What's your background? How did you get into law?"

He gave her a quick smile. "I guess turnabout is

fair play. I grew up in Tennessee, in the shadow of the Smoky Mountains. Unlike you, I had to think long and hard about leaving.''

''Why did you?''

He shrugged. ''A lot of reasons. For one thing, law seemed like a career where I could do some good, help people, advance the cause of justice. I was pretty idealistic in the early days.''

His reasons for his career choice made many of Amy's sound shallow and self-serving, she realized, and she took a sip of coffee while she mulled over his answer—especially the past tense in the last sentence. ''And you aren't idealistic anymore?''

His eyes grew troubled. ''When the system works the way it's supposed to, when I can really help someone and justice is served, it's incredibly satisfying,'' he said slowly. ''Unfortunately, that doesn't happen nearly often enough.''

''Is it happening in the Jamie Johnson case?''

''I guess we'll see when the verdict comes in.''

''But you think he's guilty.''

''I'm prosecuting him.''

''You're avoiding the question, Counselor.''

''That's right.''

She sighed. He'd easily deflected her few subtle probes about the trial during the evening. So far, she had nothing usable, no lead that would give her the edge she so badly wanted. Then again, she hadn't pressed all that hard. For some reason, her heart just hadn't been in it. Besides, it had quickly become apparent to her that while she was a good reporter who knew how to ask the right questions, he was an even better attorney who knew how to avoid answering them.

"I'm still going to try and find an angle to make my coverage stand out," she warned.

"I wish you luck." He took a final sip of his coffee, then glanced at his watch. "Well, for an evening that almost ended before it began, we've managed to make a night of it."

She checked the time and her eyes grew wide. It was after eleven. "I had no idea!"

He smiled, then rose and began clearing the table. "I promised Joe I'd have all this stuff back safe and sound tomorrow."

She stood also. "Let me help."

When everything was carefully packed, Cal lifted the box and Amy followed him to the door. He turned to her, but the simple good-night he'd planned to say stuck in his throat. Suddenly he didn't want to leave the softly lit room, where the candles cast flickering shadows on the wall in the dining alcove and sensuous jazz played quietly in the background. He drew in a slow, unsteady breath, inhaling the faint, pleasing fragrance that emanated from Amy's hair. Suddenly Cal felt warm. Too warm. He cleared his throat and shifted the box.

"Well…"

"The evening didn't turn out exactly as we planned, did it?" Amy said softly, her green eyes luminous in the golden light.

"Not quite."

"Take care of that eye."

"I will. Listen…thanks for being a good sport about the dinner."

"You were the one who was a good sport. And I had a great dinner."

"You can't go wrong with Joe's food."

Amy *had* enjoyed the food. But the dinner had been great for a lot of other reasons, she realized as she stared up at Cal. The assistant prosecuting attorney had turned out to be an incredible date, even if she hadn't gotten the hoped-for lead. In fact, this evening had been well worth the five-hundred-dollar price tag. It had been a very long time since she'd enjoyed a date this much. And the truth was, she was sorry it was over. Mostly because she knew there wouldn't be a next time.

"Well..." Cal repeated. "I guess I'd better go. It's late."

"Right."

Still he hesitated. Cal wasn't sure why. For some reason the unexpected events of the evening had thrown him off balance. And he wasn't thinking only of the mugging, he realized, as he looked into Amy's appealing green eyes. Their gazes locked for several eternal seconds, and he wished he knew what she was thinking. Was she suddenly as confused as he was? Had her pulse lurched into overdrive, too? His gaze dropped to her lips. Was she fighting the same surprising and powerful urge he was?

Cal had no idea. All he knew was that he was glad he was holding the box of dishes. Because as he said a very rapid good-night and escaped into the hall, he knew that if his arms weren't otherwise occupied, he would be very tempted to put them to another use. And he didn't think that would be wise at all.

Chapter Four

"Amy? Have I caught you at a bad time?"

Amy smiled and grabbed her tea as she headed for the couch. "Not at all. It's great to hear your voice, Kate." She sat on the couch and tucked her feet under her. "How's St. Louis?"

"It's too soon to tell, after only a week. But it doesn't matter where we live, as long as I'm with Jack."

"Still crazy in love with that handsome hunk you married, I see," Amy teased.

"Absolutely. You should try it sometime."

"Well, when I meet the right handsome hunk, I just might do that." For some reason, an image of Cal flitted through her mind, and she frowned. How odd. If ever two people had different philosophies of life, it was them. Though they did agree on some things, their basic priorities and motivations were at opposite ends of the spectrum. Not a good omen for a long-term relationship—even if they were interested in pursuing one. Which, of course, they weren't.

"I'm sure you meet all kinds of handsome men in your business," Kate scoffed.

"With egos to match, too," Amy countered dryly.

"Oh, come on. You must meet *some* guys who aren't self-centered."

Again Amy thought of Cal. "Actually, I did meet one recently."

"Well, that's more like it! Tell me all."

"I bought a date with him."

There was a beat of silence on the other end of the line before Kate spoke. "Do you want to explain that?"

Amy grinned. "I bought a date with him at a charity auction."

"You've resorted to buying dates? Things must be worse than I thought!"

This time Amy laughed. "I had an ulterior motive. He's the prosecuting attorney in a high-profile case I'm covering, and I was hoping he'd let something slip that would give me an angle."

"Oh." The disappointment in Kate's voice was obvious. "So it was just a business thing."

"Yeah. But I actually had a good time."

"Did you get your angle?"

"Unfortunately, no. But he was surprisingly pleasant, considering that we'd clashed in every previous encounter. And he was a really good sport." Amy recounted the story of the mugging.

"He sounds nice," Kate commented. "Are you sure you don't want to pursue this?"

"Trust me, Kate. I am the last person Cal Richards wants to see again. He admitted himself that he was dreading our date, so the odds of—" The ringing of the doorbell interrupted her. "Can you hold a minute? There's someone at the door."

"Sure."

Amy set her mug down and strode toward the door, pausing to peer through the peephole. All she could see was a large, green blob, so she cautiously cracked the door, leaving the chain lock in place.

A face appeared around the blob, which Amy now realized was a flower arrangement wrapped in green paper. "Amy Winter?"

"Yes."

"These are for you."

Amy gave the young man a puzzled frown. "Are you sure?"

He recited the address, and her frown deepened. "Well, you've got the right place," she conceded. She closed the door and slid the chain across, then opened it. The young man grinned and placed the vase in Amy's hands. "Enjoy."

As he disappeared down the steps, she stared at the cloud of green tissue. Who in the world would be sending her flowers?

Suddenly she remembered that Kate was waiting. Shoving the door shut with her foot, she moved quickly back to the couch, placing the vase carefully on the coffee table.

"Kate? Sorry."

"Do you need to hang up?"

"No. It was just a delivery. Flowers believe it or not."

"Flowers? Okay, sister dear, you've been holding out on me. Who are they from?"

"I haven't a clue," Amy confessed.

"There must be a card."

Amy poked at the tissue, discovered a small white envelope and rapidly scanned the note inside.

"Please accept my apologies again for the change in plans last night. And thanks for being such a good sport. Cal."

Amy stared at it, stunned. "I don't believe it!"

"What?"

"They're from Cal Richards!"

"No kidding! And this is the man who was never going to contact you again, huh?"

Amy ignored Kate's jibe and tore the paper away from the vase, letting out a soft exclamation of pleasure. "Oh, Amy, you should see this arrangement! It's gorgeous! A dozen peach-colored roses with baby's breath and fern. It's stunning!"

"Sounds like there could be potential here after all," Kate mused.

Amy looked at the card again. "It's just an apology, Kate. For the change in plans. That's what the card says. After all, I did pay five hundred dollars for that date."

"Five hundred dollars!" Now it was Kate's turn to sound incredulous. "Wow! Still, he could have sent carnations and daisies. Or just a note. Or nothing at all."

Amy fingered the card thoughtfully. "He told me

last night that he always pays his debts. I guess he felt he owed me more than an eat-in dinner.''

"He sounds like a *very* nice man, Amy."

"He is. He's just not for me," Amy declared, refusing to read more into the gesture than she was sure Cal intended. "Now tell me more about you. Are you adjusting okay since the move?"

"That was a pretty abrupt—what do you call it again in your business? A segue? But I can take a hint. Pretty well, actually, though the move is only the first in a series of adjustments."

"What do you mean?"

"I have some other news."

Amy heard the undertone of excitement in Kate's voice and held her breath. "You have my full attention."

"We're going to have a baby!"

Amy's heart soared. Kate and Jack had been trying unsuccessfully for five years to start the family they both wanted, but it had been a frustrating and disheartening process. Amy knew that over the last year Kate had begun to lose hope, had struggled to come to grips with the fact that perhaps it simply wasn't meant to be. And now this!

"Oh, Kate, I'm thrilled! When are you due?"

"October 26. I've known for a couple of weeks, but we wanted to make sure everything was okay before we told anyone."

"I bet Mom is excited."

"Ecstatic. A grandmother at last!"

They chatted excitedly for a few more minutes, but when Amy at last replaced the receiver, her euphoric mood suddenly evaporated. She was happy for Kate, of course. That went without saying. She knew how much her sister wanted a family. But she also had an odd and unexpected feeling of melancholy, which puzzled her. It wasn't as if she would want to change places with Kate. She liked her life, had worked hard to make her ambitious goals a reality and was now beginning to reap the rewards of all her hard work. But the price had been high. Too high, according to her mother, who made it a point to occasionally remind her younger daughter that her success had come at the expense of other things. Like a personal life. And a husband. And a family.

As if she didn't know, Amy thought with a sigh. She took a sip of her now-tepid tea and leaned back against the couch. It wasn't that she didn't want those things. It was just that now was not the time for them. Which didn't mean that she was immune to loneliness, she admitted. There were times when she yearned for a caring touch, or a simple, loving look, or the comfort of knowing that someone was waiting for her at the end of the day. But throughout the years she'd learned a lot about self-discipline and delayed gratification. Someday she'd go after those things, applying the same single-minded determination with which she was now pursuing her career goals. But she couldn't do both at once, and right now her career took priority.

Her gaze drifted to the roses, and she reached out to gently touch a velvety petal. She had to admit that she'd enjoyed her rare social evening last night. She'd been pleasantly surprised by Cal Richards, had begun to see him in a new and appealing light. He seemed like a decent, caring, considerate man. Under other circumstances, maybe something could have developed between them, despite their differences. But Amy didn't have the time. And she was pretty sure Cal didn't have the inclination.

"So how did the big date go on Fri—good grief! What happened to you?"

Cal glanced up at Cynthia, who was staring at him wide-eyed. "I have a black eye," he replied dryly.

"I can see that. Was there a brawl at the restaurant or something?"

"We didn't go to a restaurant. We stayed at her place and ordered in."

Cynthia's mouth dropped open. "For five hundred bucks you give her takeout? Well, that explains it. I'd have socked you, too, after paying that kind of money for a date."

Cal smiled. "That's not quite what happened."

Cynthia dropped into the chair across from his desk. "I didn't think so. Tell me everything."

"I got mugged in the parking lot of her apartment."

Once more Cynthia's eyes grew wide. "Mugged! You're kidding!"

"Those were *her* exact words when she opened the door. And, as I said then, do I *look* like I'm kidding?"

Cynthia eyed him speculatively. "I guess not. What happened?"

"Two thugs jumped me. They got my money, I got

a bloody nose and a black eye. Considering the circumstances, she very graciously consented to eat in.''

"So what did you get? Pizza?"

"You're two for two, now. Her words, again. And no, we didn't get pizza. I have a friend in the restaurant business who sent something over.''

"What restaurant?"

When he told her, she gave a low whistle. "Now *that's* a carryout! I bet the lady was impressed."

"She seemed to enjoy it."

"So…are you going to see her again?"

He looked at her in surprise. "Why would I?"

"Didn't you like her?"

Cal frowned. As a matter of fact he had—despite himself. She had many qualities that he found appealing—and intriguing. She was a woman of paradoxes—gung-ho about her career, as well as smart, savvy, ambitious and willing to push hard to get the job done, but also a woman who seemed to find aggressiveness and the in-your-face demands of her profession distasteful and who clearly had solid moral and ethical values.

However, it was equally clear that the two of them had very different priorities. Even under ideal conditions—and the fact that she was a newswoman pursuing him as a source was definitely *not* ideal—he doubted whether anything serious could ever develop between them.

"Well, if you have to think that long about it, I guess I have my answer," Cynthia said dryly. "But not to worry. We'll find you somebody yet, Cal."

Cal shook his head. "Give it up, Cyn. I don't have the time."

"You should *make* the time."

"Now you sound like my grandmother."

"I'm sure she's a very wise woman."

"She is. And you're both right. And I'll get around to it one of these days."

"Hmph. By the time you get around to it, there won't be anything left to get," she said pertly as she turned to go.

Cal watched her exit. At thirty-four, he didn't exactly consider himself over-the-hill. But he *was* well past the age when most of his friends and acquaintances had married. In fact, many of them had a couple of kids by now. Though he'd admitted it to no one, the notion of "settling down," as his grandmother would say, held more and more appeal for him these days. It would be nice to have a wife and children to come home to at the end of the day. Trouble was, his *day* often didn't end until well into the *night,* which wasn't conducive to family life. At least, not the kind of family life he wanted.

Which brought him back once again to the tough choice he was facing. Stay in the city to fight for justice and continue building his promising career, or make a radical lifestyle change and return to the mountains where his soul was most at peace. Considering his unsettled state, it wouldn't be fair to pursue a romance. Besides, only a very special woman would understand why he was discontent with his life in the city, why he was drawn so strongly to the mountains, when in the eyes of the world he seemed to have it all—success, prestige, the potential for power. And he seriously doubted whether Amy Winter was that woman.

Cal frowned. Why in the world had Amy popped into his mind again, and in such an odd context? It didn't matter in the least if she understood his motivations. Their contact in the future would be limited, and purely of a professional nature.

A week ago that scenario would have made him happy. But for some inexplicable reason, it now left him feeling vaguely depressed.

"That should do it, Steve," Amy said as she closed her notebook.

The cameraman extinguished the light and took the Minicam off his shoulder as Amy turned back to Michael Sloan, the director of the youth center.

"All we need now is some B-roll footage as background," she said. "Can we do a walk-through, see some of the activities in progress?"

"Sure." He rose and led them down the hall to a small but well-equipped computer lab. Boys ranging in age from seven or eight to mid-teens were using every available piece of equipment under the supervision of an older man, who smiled at them when they entered.

"That's John Williams, one of the volunteers," the director told Amy. "As I mentioned earlier, our volunteers are the backbone of this place. They not only provide much-needed manpower, but act as great role models for the boys, many of whom are from broken homes without a father figure."

He introduced Amy to the volunteer, and with the man's consent, she spoke with him for a few minutes on camera.

They stopped in a few other rooms, where a variety of activities, from woodworking and drawing to rehearsal for a theater production, were in progress.

"The other big part of our program is sports," Michael told her as he ushered them down the hall toward the gym. "We have athletic activities scheduled every night. Tonight it's basketball, and we are incredibly fortunate to have a prominent local attorney as one of our coaches. He's working with the youngteen team right now. He's a bit camera-shy, but I'll see what I can do to convince him to give you an interview."

Amy frowned. An attorney. Camera shy. Saint Vincent's Boy's Club. Her step faltered. Wasn't Saint Vincent's the charity Candace Bryce had referenced when she introduced Cal at the charity bachelor auction? Hadn't she said something about him participating only because Saint Vincent's would benefit? Amy hadn't made the connection until now. But surely there were other attorneys who volunteered here, she reassured herself. It would be too much of a coincidence if he happened to be here the very night she'd come to do her story. Yet somehow, deep inside, she sensed that, coincidence or not, it was him.

Amy's heart began to pound. She didn't want to intrude on Cal's off-duty "turf." It was too...well, personal. Since their "date" two weeks before, their only contact had been in the courtroom, and then only an occasional, fleeting connecting of gazes. He hadn't acknowledged the thank-you note she'd sent him for the flowers, nor had she expected him to. Their limited contact had been impersonal and therefore safe. Which was fine with her. Something strange had happened that night as he was leaving her apartment. The unexpected sizzle of electricity that had sparked between them had left her rattled. For whatever reason, Cal Richards was a distraction, and distractions were not something she needed at this point in her career.

Michael stopped at the gym door and pushed it open for her to enter. "A lot of the boys in here would be on the streets if it wasn't for people like Cal Richards," he said, confirming Amy's premonition.

Her heart stopped, then raced on. She hesitated, and both the director and Steve looked at her questioningly.

"Something wrong, Amy?" Steve asked.

She forced herself to take a deep breath. She knew her reaction was totally illogical. After all, she'd covered any number of stories that had put her in physical danger or resulted in threats of bodily harm, and she'd always remained calm and cool. This situation was a piece of cake compared to that. She could handle this, she told herself reassuringly.

But as she stepped to the door, the sight of Cal in his tank T-shirt and sweatpants, with biceps to rival a Mr. World candidate she'd once interviewed, made her long for the relative safety of a bank robbery or an impending tornado. However, since both Steve and Michael were staring at her curiously, she was left with no choice but to enter the gym.

"Just taking a moment to observe," she replied

belatedly to Steve's question. His skeptical look as she brushed past told her he didn't buy her response, but it was the best she could do.

"I'll see what I can do about that interview," Michael said. "Excuse me for just a minute."

"So what gives?" Steve asked the moment the director was out of earshot.

Amy gazed after Michael as he headed toward the group of boys clustered around Cal. "It's just that the assistant prosecuting attorney and I have…clashed…a few times."

Steve followed her gaze. "You and every other member of the press in Atlanta. Join the club. Haven't you given up on him yet?"

"I don't give up," Amy said determinedly. "I still go to the courthouse almost every day. But so far, no luck."

Just then Cal looked her way, and their gazes met for one brief moment before he turned back to Michael and said a few words. Then he directed his attention to the boys, and Michael rejoined them.

"No luck on the interview, I'm afraid," he apologized. "Cal's one of our biggest supporters—in a lot of ways—but he keeps it low-profile. His motives are purely altruistic, and he has no interest in personal recognition or accolades. However, when I explained to him that this feature would be good for Saint Vincent's and might encourage others to support our work, he did agree to some—what did you call it— B-roll filming?"

"That will be fine, Michael," Amy assured him.

"I think we have plenty of other shots, so we'll just film for a few minutes here and then wrap it up."

"Great." He glanced at his watch and frowned. "I hate to run, but my daughter is in a school play tonight, and I'll just be able to make it if I leave now. Would you mind if I took off while you finish up?"

"Not at all," Amy assured him. "Thank you for your help."

"Thank *you*," he replied, shaking her hand. "You can't imagine how much this kind of publicity will mean to Saint Vincent's."

"I hope so. You do good work here, and you deserve all the support you can get."

"Thanks." He shook hands with Steve, as well. "Feel free to spend as much time as you like here. Cal just asked that you try to keep him in the background as much as possible when you film."

"No problem," Steve assured him, hoisting his Minicam into position.

"I'll wait over there," Amy said, nodding toward the corner where a youngster sat alone on a folding chair, watching them curiously. "Good night, Michael."

"Good night."

As Steve scoped out the gym for angles, Amy wandered over to the little boy of about seven, who was sitting on his hands, his legs wrapped around the legs of the chair. She sat beside him and smiled.

"Hi. My name's Amy. What's yours?"

"Mark." He spoke softly and hung his head.

"Well, it's nice to meet you, Mark." She nodded toward the court. "Do you play basketball?"

He shook his head. "I'm too little."

"But not for long. Pretty soon you'll be just as big as those guys out there."

He looked up at her shyly. "I hope I can play as good as my brother. He's on the team. Mr. Richards says I have po-po-potential."

He struggled with the complicated word, and Amy smiled. "Then I'm sure you do."

"Mr. Richards lets me watch. He says I can learn a lot by watching. And sometimes, when the practice is over, he shows me how to hold the ball and how to throw."

"Sounds like he's very nice."

Mark nodded vigorously. "I like to talk to him. He listens real good." Mark glanced toward Steve. "What's he doing?"

"He's shooting some video for a story we're going to do on the news about Saint Vincent's."

"Wow! You mean we're going to be on TV?"

"Yes."

"How come?"

"Because Saint Vincent's is a good place, and we want to let other people know about it."

"I like it here," Mark affirmed. "Sometimes it's not real nice at home, when my mom is sick, so Troy—that's my brother—and I come here and do stuff."

"That should be a wrap, Amy. You want anything else?"

She looked up at Steve. "I think we're done. Thanks, Steve."

"No problem. Want me to walk you to your car?"

"Sure." Saint Vincent's wasn't in the safest neighborhood, and Amy didn't take unnecessary chances.

"Let me just check in and see where I need to go next."

"Do you want to use my phone?" She reached for her purse, but he shook his head.

"Mine's in the bag. I'll stow this stuff, then call. Just give me a couple of minutes."

Amy turned back to Mark. "So you like coming to Saint Vincent's?"

He nodded emphatically. "It's neat. After school they give us cookies and milk. And the grown-ups here don't yell or throw things or anything. They talk nice to us and listen to what we say, like we're important. It makes me feel good to come here."

Amy leaned closer and laid her hand on his. "You know something, Mark? You *are* important. Every person is different, and every single one is important in his own way. There's nobody else in the whole world just like you, and nobody could ever take your place. You remember that, okay?"

Mark smiled shyly. "You're nice, Amy. I wish my mom talked like you."

"Ready to do a little practicing, Mark?"

Mark and Amy simultaneously looked up at Cal. She was glad for Mark's eager response, which momentarily distracted Cal, because for a second her voice deserted her. It was one thing to look at Cal in his workout clothes from across the gym, and quite another to have him standing only two feet away. His tank T-shirt clung to his broad chest, and with one hand on his hip and the other arm hugging the basketball to his side, his well-defined biceps made her breath catch in her throat. The man was in absolutely perfect physical condition, she realized, from his pecs to his abs. There wasn't an ounce of excess flesh on his well-toned body. Muscled chest, tapering waist, flat stomach, slim hips. To use one of Darlene's favorite expressions, Cal Richards was one hot-looking dude. If during their date she'd been impressed by the man's mind and ethics, today she was equally impressed by his physical attributes. He radiated a virility that literally took her breath away and made her respiration go haywire.

As Cal finished his brief conversation with Mark, handed him the ball and watched him scamper off, Amy reached for her purse and made a pretense of looking for her keys, trying to buy herself a few moments to restore her poise. No man had ever wreaked such havoc on her emotional and physical equilibrium by his mere proximity. That Cal Richards should be the one man who *could* seemed like a nasty trick of fate. Why couldn't some *compatible* man have had this effect on her—and about two or three years down the road?

Cal turned back to Amy, planted his hands on his hips and took a moment to study her bowed head as she searched through her purse. Her light brown hair swung forward, hiding her face, and he was glad for the momentary reprieve. He hadn't planned to speak to her. But as he'd watched her interact with Mark, he'd been struck by the quick rapport she'd established with the shy little boy, who—for good reason—had a real problem with trust and rarely said more than a few words to strangers. The fact that she had quickly broken through his reserve and established a comfort level with him said a lot. It was yet another appealing side of this intriguing woman, and he'd found himself walking over to her without making a conscious decision to do so.

Amy withdrew her keys and slung her purse over her shoulder before she looked up.

"Hello, Cal."

Her voice seemed more throaty than usual, and he suddenly found it difficult to swallow. "Hello, Amy. This is a surprise. Isn't this a bit off your normal beat?"

She shrugged. "I go where the stories are."

He glanced at his watch. "How many hours a day do you work? You were in court at nine this morning."

She looked at him steadily. "How ever many it takes."

He frowned. "But why would they assign you to two stories twelve hours apart?"

"They didn't assign this one. I proposed it and got permission to put a piece together. I'm hoping it's good enough to win airtime. But the rest of my work still needs to get done. So I do these kinds of stories after hours."

His frown deepened. "Have you had dinner?"

The impulsive question surprised him as much as it obviously did her.

"No."

He hesitated, unsure what had prompted that query. But he was in too far now to back out, and he didn't have time to analyze his motives. "Would you like to grab a bite with me? I came here directly from the office, and I'm starving."

She stared at him. Was he actually *initiating* a date? With a woman he'd gone to great lengths to avoid? "Could you repeat that? I think my ears are playing tricks on me," she said cautiously.

Cal gave her a crooked grin. "Would you believe me if I told you I'm as surprised by the invitation as you are?"

She couldn't doubt the sincerity in his eyes. "Yes."

"So how about it?"

She tilted her head and looked at him quizzically. "Can I ask why?"

He paused to consider. "That's a fair—but tough—question," he replied candidly. "Frankly I have no idea. Maybe because I feel I still owe you a dinner. Maybe because I enjoyed our evening together. Maybe because it would make my grandmother happy."

She eyed him warily, but now there was a slight twinkle in her eye. "I'm not even going to ask about that last reason."

"Good. So?"

She studied him for another few seconds, then gave a slight shrug. "Why not?"

He smiled, and the warmth in his eyes brought a flush to her cheeks. "Great. Give me ten minutes to shower and change."

Cal headed back toward the boys still on the court as Amy stared after him.

"What was that all about?"

With an effort she tore her gaze from Cal's retreating figure and looked up to find that Steve had returned. "He asked me out to dinner."

Steve's eyebrows rose. "No kidding! What brought that on?"

"I have no idea."

"Well, maybe it will give you a chance to pump him for that angle you're after."

"Maybe."

But oddly enough, for a woman who always put business first, the very last thing on her mind at the moment was the Jamie Johnson trial.

Chapter Five

By the time Cal reappeared fresh from the shower exactly ten minutes later—looking fabulous in worn jeans that fit like a glove, a cotton shirt with the long sleeves rolled back to the elbows and his wet hair even darker than usual—the modicum of poise Amy had regained during his absence immediately evaporated.

"Right on time," she remarked breathlessly, glancing at her watch as she struggled to control the sudden staccato beat of her heart.

"My grandmother always told me never to keep a pretty lady waiting," Cal said with a wink, which did nothing to restore her equilibrium.

She was glad he wasn't privy to her elevated pulse rate—although there was nothing she could do to hide the telltale flush that suffused her face at the unexpected compliment. "I think I like your grandmother," she replied, struggling for a light tone.

He chuckled. "She's a hard lady not to like. Ready?"

Amy nodded, and Cal fell into step beside her as they headed for the exit.

"Is she still in Tennessee?" Amy asked.

"Yes. Always has been, always will be."

"By choice or circumstance?"

"Choice. She's perfectly content with her cabin in the mountains and her work at the local craft co-op."

When they reached the door, Cal pushed it open, one hand in the small of her back as he guided her out. It was an impersonal gesture, born of breeding and good manners, but it nevertheless sent a tingle up her spine. Get a grip, Amy admonished herself. It's okay to enjoy this impromptu date, but remember—there's no future here. You are two very different people.

"Where are you parked?" Cal asked as he surveyed the small lot.

Amy pointed toward a late-model BMW. "Over there."

Cal noted the car, but made no comment. Instead, he turned to her, his gaze moving swiftly over her attire, taking in the royal blue jacket with black buttons, wide gold choker, black slacks and heels. "Where would you like to go? You're dressed for the Ritz, but I don't think they'd even let me in the back door," he said with an engaging grin.

She smiled and shrugged. "Anywhere is fine. Fast food, if you like."

"Oh, I think we can do a little better than that. Have you ever eaten at Rick's?"

"No."

"It's a nice place—good food, comfortable atmosphere. And not too far from your apartment, so it will be convenient."

"For me, maybe. But what about you? I'm sure your day has been as long as mine. How about somewhere in between our places?" Amy countered. "Where do you live?"

He named the modest suburb—a far cry from her upscale neighborhood. Considering his position, she was a bit surprised—but not too much. She was beginning to realize that Cal Richards was a man who preferred a simple life and didn't have a pretentious bone in his body.

"Frankly, unless you have some other preference, I'd enjoy going to Rick's. It would be a nice change of pace. By the time I get around to dinner most nights I'm too tired to go out, so I usually just nuke something."

Amy acquiesced. "That's fine with me, then. I'll just follow you."

He waited until she was in her car, with the doors locked, before he headed to his own. She watched in the rearview mirror, and wasn't the least bit surprised when he stopped beside an older-model compact. Despite his prestigious position, Cal Richards obviously saw no need for conspicuous displays of success. The man continued to amaze—and impress—her.

When they arrived at the restaurant, he was out of his car and beside her door almost before she turned off the motor. As she reached for her purse and stepped out, she smiled. "My compliments to your mother. She obviously raised a gentleman."

Though he smiled in response, a fleeting pain passed across his eyes. "Actually, my grandmother gets most of the credit. My mom died when I was twelve."

Amy's gaze softened in sympathy. "I'm sorry."

"Thanks. It was a hard time for everyone. Dad was beside himself, so Gram suggested we move in with her until we got past the worst of the grief. It worked out so well, we never left. I always missed Mom, of course, but Gram was great. She did a terrific job as a surrogate mother. And Dad went above and beyond, trying to make up for the fact that I only had one parent. I don't think he ever missed a single event in my life, from spelling bees to camping trips with the Scouts."

"I take it the three of you are still close."

"Very." He ushered her inside the restaurant, and smiled at the hostess. "Hello, Steph."

"Cal! It's good to see you. It's been too long."

"Tell me about it," he said ruefully. "Life's too busy. But I'm overdue for a dose of Rick's cooking."

She picked up two menus and led the way to a quiet corner table. "I'll let him know you're here. Enjoy."

Once they were seated, he took one brief glance at the menu then laid it aside.

"A man of quick decision, I see," Amy remarked.

He flashed her a grin. "No, just in a rut. I always seem to get the same thing here."

"Which is?"

"Seafood pasta and the house salad. It's a pretty tough combination to beat."

Amy put her menu down. "You convinced me."

A moment later the waiter arrived with a basket of crusty French bread still warm from the oven, and Amy helped herself while Cal gave their order. She closed her eyes and smiled as she took the first bite.

"Now *this* is the way to end a long day," she declared.

Cal chuckled and followed her example. "It sure beats a microwave dinner."

"Amen to that," she replied fervently. "Unfortunately, that's my usual fare."

He smiled. "I take it the kitchen isn't your favorite room."

She tilted her head and considered the question. "Actually, I *like* to cook. But there's never any time."

"That commodity does seem to be in short supply these days," he agreed with a sigh.

"Yet you manage to find time to help out at Saint Vincent's."

He shrugged dismissively. "A lot of people do a lot more."

"Maybe they're not as busy as you are."

"Some are busier. And the basketball is only one night a week."

"Michael Sloan hinted that your support went way beyond that."

Cal shifted uncomfortably. "I help out here and there in different ways," he said vaguely. "I believe in the work they do. Those kids need all the help and encouragement they can get. I've been very blessed, and I feel the need to give something back, to demonstrate my gratitude in a concrete way. Saint Vincent's lets me do that.''

He made it sound as if Saint Vincent's was doing *him* a favor, she thought, once again impressed by the way he downplayed his obviously significant contribution to the boys' center. ''You certainly have a fan in Mark,'' she observed.

Cal smiled briefly, then grew more serious. ''Mark's a great kid. He's smart, ambitious and willing to learn. Which is saying a lot, considering he comes from a single-parent home headed by an alcoholic mother, has no idea who his father is and lives in one of the poorest—and roughest—sections of the city. He and his brother are the kind of kids we're trying to help at Saint Vincent's. We want them to understand that they *do* have options and that there are people who care.''

''You seem to be doing a good job of it, to hear Mark talk. How did you get involved there, anyway?''

''Through my church. We sponsor an annual field trip for the kids, and I volunteered a few years ago. I've been helping out down there ever since.''

Amy tilted her head and studied him. ''So you're a churchgoing man.''

He nodded. ''All my life.''

Their salads arrived, giving her time to digest his comment. ''I admire that,'' she said frankly when the waiter departed. ''In fact, I envy it a little.''

''You don't go to church?''

"Not much anymore. We went every Sunday when I was growing up. But once I was out on my own—I don't know, other things somehow took precedence. Time was at more and more of a premium, and somehow religion dropped to the bottom of my priority list."

"That can happen," Cal said without censure. "When I first came to Atlanta I was tempted to skip church. It was just one more obligation to fit into a schedule that was already too packed. But every time I missed a Sunday, I felt somehow out of sync for the rest of the week. I know going to church is just an outward sign of faith, but it reminds me to keep my priorities straight and helps keep me grounded." He paused and studied her for a moment. "Can I ask you something?"

"Sure."

"Since you attended church most of your life, do you ever miss it now that you've stopped going?"

Amy propped her chin in her hand and considered the question. "Sometimes I feel guilty about not going. But I can't say I *miss* it, per se." She did, on occasion, however, sense that something was *missing* from her life. And she suspected it had to do with her lapsed faith. In some vague way she felt she had disappointed God, and the longer she stayed away from church, the harder it became to go back. But she wasn't about to reveal that to Cal. "I really don't think about it too often," she finished. "And I certainly don't live it the way you do."

"I don't know. Look at the story you were working on tonight. That will help a lot of people."

"I'd like to say I did it for purely selfless reasons. But my motives weren't really altruistic," she said frankly. "Yes, I hope the story benefits Saint Vincent's. But I also hope it gets me noticed."

Cal studied her for a moment. "Can I ask you something else?"

There was something in his tone that made her cautious. "Maybe."

"Are you ever off duty?"

"Of course. I'm not working right now."

"Are you sure?"

"What do you mean?"

He steepled his fingers and gave her a direct look. "I guess I'm wondering if you're still hoping to get something from me you can use in the Jamie Johnson coverage."

Amy stared at him, her fork frozen halfway to her mouth. "You think I accepted your invitation just because of that?"

He shrugged. "I can't think of any other reason. Not that I'm complaining, you understand." He gave her a wry smile. "It beats eating alone."

Amy continued to stare at him as the waiter refilled their water glasses. He couldn't think of any other reason? Was he kidding? She could think of about a dozen without even trying. He was intelligent, handsome, articulate, generous, had a good sense of humor and, considering his comment, was obviously completely without ego—a refreshing attribute and a definite plus as far as she was concerned.

Amy laid her fork down carefully and cleared her throat. "Look, I know you think I'm a workaholic, and that everything I do has an ulterior motive, but will you believe me when I say that my only reason for accepting your invitation tonight was because I wanted to? Because I enjoyed our last evening together? And because, like you, I prefer not to always eat alone?''

He chose to focus on her last comment. "If you eat alone, it must be by choice. I can't believe you lack for male companionship.''

She shrugged indifferently, pleased nonetheless by the backhanded compliment. "Relationships are demanding. And I don't have the time. So why start something I know will simply fizzle out as soon as the guy realizes he takes second place to my career?''

"Your job is that important to you? So important that you're willing to give up your personal life?''

She grimaced. "Now you sound like my mother.''

"And what do you tell her when she makes those kinds of comments?''

"That of course I want a husband. And children. But marriage and kids aren't compatible with the demands of my career. I'll get around to those things eventually.''

"After you do all the 'important stuff'?''

She gave him a startled look, then frowned. "I didn't say that. And besides, who are you to talk? You spend an inordinate amount of time at your job, too, and as far as I know you haven't made time for a wife or family, either.''

He couldn't argue with her on that. And they were heading toward turf he preferred to avoid.

"Touché," he replied lightly. "How did we get on this subject, anyway?"

Amy shook her head. "I have no idea."

"How about we get off it?"

"Good idea. I don't want to end the evening with indigestion. So...tell me what you do for fun."

"I'm not sure I remember," he confessed, a smile playing at the corners of his mouth as he chased an elusive piece of lettuce around his plate.

She rolled her eyes. "See? You *are* as bad as I am. Well...what about vacations, then? Where do you go when you manage to get away?"

"Back to the mountains."

"Honestly?"

"Yes. I've been other places, but there isn't much that can rival a morning in the Smoky Mountains, with the mist floating over the valleys and the blue-hued mountains forming an ethereal backdrop. The majesty of it never fails to take my breath away. And the incredible peace there—it's a balm for the soul."

Amy hadn't expected such a poetic description from an assistant prosecuting attorney—nor one so heartfelt. "I can see now why you said you had to think long and hard about leaving," she said slowly. "I can hear in your voice how much you love it there."

He shrugged, suddenly self-conscious. He was rarely so open in expressing his feelings about the mountains, and he wasn't sure what had prompted him to be so candid tonight. "So where do you go?" he asked, turning the tables.

"Cancún. The Caribbean. Europe now and then."

"Ah...a world traveler. What's your favorite place?"

She considered his question as the waiter replaced their salad bowls with heaping plates of pasta. "You know, I don't think I've found it yet," she replied thoughtfully. "I guess I'm still searching for the ideal spot."

As the meal progressed, they hopscotched around a half-dozen topics, deliberately staying on safe subjects. When they finally left the restaurant, long after most of the other diners had departed, he walked her to her car.

"So when will the piece on Saint Vincent's air?"

"It's not 'when,' but 'if,'" she reminded him. "It was done on a purely speculative basis. But if they're going to use it, it will probably be in the next couple of weeks on a slow news night. Most likely the six o'clock program. I'd offer to alert you, but I probably won't know until right before it airs that it's going to run."

"Well, I'll just have to keep an eye out for it, then."

Amy tossed her purse onto the passenger seat and straightened up to look at Cal. He was leaning against her door, one arm draped over the top, the other hand in his pocket, and his brown eyes were friendly and warm. More than warm, actually. If she didn't know better, she'd almost think the man was *attracted* to her. Considering the cool treatment he'd given her during their first few encounters, it was quite a transition. In fact, it was hard to believe that this was the same unfriendly man she'd approached on the courthouse steps just a few weeks before.

"Thanks for joining me tonight," he said quietly, the unusually husky cadence in his voice playing havoc with her metabolism.

"Thanks for asking me. I just wish you had let me pay for my own dinner."

"I owed you this one, remember?"

"The debt was paid in full that night at my apartment," she said firmly. "The 'takeout' you produced was five-star. And then, to top it off, you sent flowers. We're more than even, Cal."

For a moment there was silence. Cal knew that it was time to say good-night. But as he gazed down into Amy's expressive green eyes, he was suddenly reluctant for the evening to end. It was the same feeling he'd experienced that night at her apartment when it came time to leave. He hadn't understood it then, and he didn't understand it now. He shouldn't feel this way about her. Each time their paths crossed, it became more evident that their priorities in life were completely different. She drove a late-model BMW, he drove an older compact. She lived in the high-rent district, he lived in a middle-class neighborhood. She went to exotic places on vacation, he went home to Appalachia. She thrived on the fast pace of life in the city, he yearned for the slower pace of the mountains. It was obvious that there was no way on earth they could ever get together.

And yet…as he stared down at her, his heart said differently. As illogical as it seemed, he intuitively sensed that, at their core, they were more alike than either realized. Given the opportunity to really get to know each other, they might find a surprising amount of common ground.

As a rule, he didn't put much stock in intuition. It didn't always reflect reality. But one thing *was* very real—the electric attraction between them. On a purely physical level, at least, they were compatible. He could see it in her eyes, in the pulse that beat in the hollow of her throat, in the white-knuckled grip she had on her keys.

Cal drew a shaky breath. Heaven help him, but he wanted to kiss her. To deny the impulse would be foolish. But to do anything about it would be even more foolish. The lady wasn't interested in romance—with anyone. She'd made that clear tonight. And neither was he. The time just wasn't right.

Calling on every ounce of his willpower, Cal resolutely stepped back, jammed his hands in his pockets and somehow summoned up a crooked smile. "Okay. If you say so. I just want to make sure you got your five hundred dollars' worth."

If you only knew! Amy thought fervently, her gaze locked on his. Even without the hoped-for angle for her coverage, she didn't regret one dime she'd spent. Cal Richards had given her two wonderful evenings that she knew would linger long in her memory. "Trust me, Cal. We're even." She tried for a nonchalant tone, but couldn't quite control the slight quaver in her voice.

Again there was silence, and Amy had the disconcerting feeling that Cal knew exactly what was going through her mind. But if he did, he made no comment. "I'll take your word for it. Drive safely."

"I will. And thanks again."

She slipped inside the car, and he shut the door firmly behind her. With one final wave, she put the engine in gear and drove away.

Cal watched her taillights disappear into the night, then turned and slowly walked to his car. He didn't understand the attraction he felt for Amy Winter. It defied all logic. But he did understand one thing. There was a lot more to her than he'd first thought. And the more he found out about her, the more he realized that she was one unforgettable woman.

For the first time in his life, Cal made it a point to watch the six o'clock news on Amy's station, even if he had to duck into the conference room at the office to do so. He told himself it was because he was hoping to see the Saint Vincent's story. But in his heart, he knew it was because he wanted to see *Amy*.

As one week passed, then two, Saint Vincent's never made the news. But other stories by Amy did, including several that related to the Jamie Johnson trial. She continued to attend at least part of the court session each day, and she had an uncanny knack for distilling the essence of what transpired and communicating it to viewers in a straightforward way. He had to admit that her professional and balanced coverage was impressive.

But what impressed him even more was how she used the trial story to delve more deeply into related issues. One day she supplemented her trial coverage by including an interview with alcohol-abuse experts. Another day she talked with families of drunk-driving victims about the devastating impact the tragedy had had on their lives. She interviewed a psychologist, who discussed the "sports star" phenomenon and the sense of invulnerability many athletes had. And she spoke with the person who ran the homeless shelter where the victim had spent time, using it as an opportunity to create sympathetic awareness of a world with which few people ever had any direct contact.

So when the story on Saint Vincent's finally aired, he wasn't surprised to see that she had gone one step beyond on that coverage, too. Not only had she interviewed Michael and others at the center, but she'd fleshed out her coverage by talking with social workers, law-enforcement officials and educators about the plight of youngsters like Mark and the odds they had to overcome. Her coverage made it clear that these kids needed as much help and support as they could get to break free of the cycle of poverty, gangs and violence, and that Saint Vincent's was doing a stellar job providing just such support.

When the segment ended, Cal rose and slowly walked back to his office, pausing to stare out his window into the darkness. Over the past couple of weeks, two significant things had occurred. First, he'd developed a deep admiration for Amy's skill and sensitivity as a reporter. And second, he'd realized that she wasn't just good at what she did; she was exceptional. He thought back to the way he'd railed at her when they first met, how he'd made sweeping generalizations about the press, and his face grew warm.

Although his overall opinion of the news media might be valid, based on personal experience, he hadn't allowed for exceptions. And Amy was clearly an exception.

Cal wanted to call and compliment her on the Saint Vincent's story. But he wasn't sure that was wise. Because even with no contact, he'd thought way too much about her over the past two weeks. For a man known to colleagues for his powers of concentration, he'd drawn more than a few curious looks at several meetings when he'd had to ask someone to repeat a question. Cynthia had begun asking him if he was feeling all right. Bill Jackson had good-naturedly speculated about why he was so distracted and come a little too close to the truth. Even his boss had commented that after this trial, maybe he should take a vacation.

He sighed and reached around to rub the tense muscles in his neck. Despite the fact that she was a newswoman, despite the fact that they seemed to be complete opposites, despite the fact that this *wasn't* the right time in his life for romantic involvements, he was attracted to Amy Winter. Though he'd dated plenty of women throughout the years, none had been memorable enough to disrupt his focus and his concentration. His analytical, logical mind had always been able to control his heart. But not this time. Bottom line, Amy had gotten under his skin, and he didn't have a clue what to do about it.

By the time Cal walked through the door of his apartment two hours later, he was wrestling with yet another problem. In the past, he had steadfastly followed one simple rule in dealing with the press: no contact and no comment. He'd already blown the "no contact" part with Amy. And now he was actually toying with the idea of waiving the "no comment" part, too. Tomorrow he would be questioning a newly discovered witness who had information the defense wasn't going to like. Thanks to the persistence of one dedicated detective who just wouldn't rest until every angle had been explored, an eyewitness to the "accident" had been found. And his story made it clear that the victim was blameless, that Jamie Johnson had run a stop sign at a high speed and hit the pedestrian just as he reached the middle of the crosswalk. Bringing the man forward was a calculated risk, because Cal knew the man's credibility was vulnerable if the defense dug deeply enough. He hoped they wouldn't. But either way, the witness was newsworthy.

Cal figured that Amy would be in court, anyway. She'd rarely missed a session. But on the off chance she might be pulled on to another story, Cal was tempted to suggest she stick close. After all, if anyone deserved to get this "scoop," it was her. The other reporters hadn't shown up in person since the opening day, relying on daily updates issued by Johnson's agent for their coverage. What could it hurt to suggest that she might want to be in court tomorrow?

With a sigh he reached for the phone. Maybe he should just call her and play it by ear. But instead of dialing Amy's number, he found himself punching the familiar Tennessee area code. He paused, then continued dialing. Not a bad idea, he mused. Gram might be a good sounding board.

She picked up on the second ring. "You must be sitting right by the phone," he said with a smile.

"Cal? Land, I didn't expect to hear from you tonight! How are you, son?"

"Good. How are things at home?"

"Couldn't be better. The craft co-op is going gangbusters, and your dad is busy as a beaver on the church picnic committee. He's at a meeting tonight, in fact."

"I'd like to make the picnic this year," Cal said wistfully as he switched the portable phone to the other hand and slid a frozen dinner into the microwave. "Do they still put on that great spread, with homemade apple butter and Moira Sanders's biscuits?"

"Of course. And speaking of food, did I just hear you turn on the microwave for one of those processed dinners?"

Cal chuckled and straddled a stool at the eat-in counter in his galley kitchen. You couldn't put anything past Gram, even from two hundred and fifty miles away. "Guilty."

"Is that the way you eat every night?"

He thought of his last dinner with Amy. "No. Sometimes I go out. I had a good dinner two weeks ago, in fact."

"With good company, too, I hope?"

"Mmm-hmm."

For a moment there was silence, and then he heard her sigh. "Cal Richards, you are the most closemouthed man I ever met! Can't imagine where you get it from. Do I have to pry every piece of information out of you?'' she complained good-naturedly.

He chuckled again. ''If you're trying to find out whether my companion was female, the answer is yes.''

''That newswoman you told me about?'' she asked shrewdly.

''Yes. But don't get your hopes up, Gram. It was an impromptu thing. She was doing a story on Saint Vincent's, and I coincidentally happened to be there that night. We just grabbed a bite afterward. It was no big deal.''

''She must be nice, though, or you wouldn't have suggested dinner.''

''Yes, she is. Surprisingly so. When I first met her, I thought she was the typical pushy, 'go-for-the-sensational' reporter, but I've been impressed by her coverage. She's gone above and beyond to present a balanced picture of all the issues surrounding the trial. Which, in one way, has created a bit of a dilemma for me.''

''How do you mean?''

''Well, there's something breaking tomorrow, and if anyone deserves a first shot at it, she does. None of the other reporters have even come close to providing the comprehensive coverage she has. Trouble is, there's a chance she might not be in court, and if she's not there she won't get the scoop.''

''So call her up and tell her to be there.''

He sighed. ''It's not quite that simple, Gram. I've always made it a rule to steer clear of reporters, and

I never give tips. Ethically I'm not sure I should make an exception.''

"How is suggesting she be in court giving her a tip?''

"She'll put two and two together and figure out something is going to break. She's one sharp lady.''

"Well, remember the old saying about rules, Cal. And there are extenuating circumstances here. You said yourself she deserves this scoop.''

"Yeah. I'm just having a hard time being objective about this. I don't want to let personal feelings get in the way of good judgment.''

"So…you have personal feelings for this woman?''

Cal frowned. He should have chosen his words more carefully. Gram was one sharp lady herself. "I hardly know her, Gram,'' he hedged.

"Hmm. Well, far as I can see, there's nothing wrong with giving a deserving person a break. The news will get out either way. Might as well be from her.''

She made it sound simple, Cal thought. And maybe it was. Maybe he was making way too much out of this. After all, he wasn't going to tell Amy anything. He just wanted to make sure she was in court to get the news when it did break. "Thanks, Gram.''

"For what?''

"For helping me decide what to do.''

"Well, it just seems like common sense to me. It's not like you're giving away a state secret.''

Cal chuckled. "True. Listen, tell Dad I said hi, okay?''

"Will do. And, Cal? Do one thing for me, would you?"

"What?"

"Work on those personal feelings. You never know where they might lead."

"I'll give it some thought."

"Don't think too much, son. You have a fine mind. But some things are best left to the heart."

As Cal replaced the receiver a few moments later, he thought about his grandmother's advice. She might be right—but he wasn't sure he trusted his heart in this case. There were just too many odds stacked against a relationship between him and Amy. Yet, even as logic told him not to take the chance, his heart urged him to do otherwise.

Cal sighed. He didn't know which would triumph in the end, but he did know one thing. Ready or not, bad timing notwithstanding, incompatibilities aside, he had suddenly come face-to-face with an opportunity for romance. And he had a feeling that it was about to change his life forever.

Chapter Six

Amy glanced over at Cal. He'd only looked her way once since the afternoon court session began. But that one look, along with an undercurrent of tension in the courtroom, convinced her that something big was about to break.

As she studied his strong profile, she thought again about his unexpected call the night before. Though he'd complimented her on the Saint Vincent's story, it had been clear that his main purpose was to ensure that she would be in court today. Considering his impeccable integrity and "no comment" policy with the press, she suspected that he'd wrestled with the decision about whether to call her. The fact that he *had* made her feel…well, lots of things. And most of them didn't have a thing to do with the trial. Sure, her adrenaline was pumping, as it always did when she was covering a story that had potential for high drama. But the warm glow in her heart and the anticipatory tingle in her nerve endings had no connection to her job.

Knowing that Cal had come to respect and like her enough to stretch the limits of his ethics on her behalf made her feel very good—not to mention more than a little nervous. Although their relationship had started out rocky, and despite the fact that they were different in so many ways, she liked Cal Richards. A lot. Which wasn't wise, of course. Cal and she obviously weren't right for each other. And besides, she didn't have time for romance. She had a career to build, and that took every ounce of her energy and focus. She couldn't afford any distractions. And the assistant prosecuting attorney was a distraction with a capital *D*.

"The prosecution would like to call Eldon Lewis to the stand."

Amy refocused her attention on the courtroom proceedings. As she watched the older man make his way to the witness stand, she sensed that he was the reason Cal had called her. She leaned forward intently, watching as the man took the oath and sat down.

Cal walked over and smiled at the witness, who was clearly nervous.

"Mr. Lewis, would you please state your name and occupation for the court?" His stance was relaxed, his tone conversational, and Amy knew he was trying to put the man at ease.

"Eldon Lewis. I'm a janitor at the community college."

"And what do you enjoy doing in your free time, Mr. Lewis?"

"I'm a big sports fan."

"So you're familiar with the defendant in this case, Jamie Johnson?"

The man darted a quick glance at the sports star. "Yeah. He's a real good player."

"I want you to think back to last September. Can you tell the court what you did on the night of September fourth?"

The man swallowed and nodded. "Me and my friend Hal went to the game. Jamie was playing that night. After the game, we stopped at the Watering Hole by the stadium to get a burger."

"What time did you leave?"

"About one in the morning."

"Can you tell us what you saw when you were leaving?"

"Well, I waited in front while my friend went to get the car. I have a bum leg, and it was acting up that night. I was kind of back in the shadows, and next thing I know, Jamie Johnson pulls up at the bar next door. A girl got out of his car, and they were laughing." The man paused and shifted uncomfortably.

"Are you sure it was Jamie Johnson, Mr. Lewis?" Cal asked, his tone still conversational.

The man nodded emphatically. "Sure. He got out of the car to open her door, and the streetlight was shining right on his face. Then he kind of tripped on the curb, and he and the girl started laughing again. She called him 'Jamie' when she said good-night, and she told him to drive careful because the last thing he needed was a drunk-driving charge."

A murmur swept the courtroom, and the judge banged his gavel until order was restored.

Cal waited until the room was completely quiet before he spoke again. "Please continue, Mr. Lewis. What happened next?"

"After the girl went in, Jamie got back in the car and took off with his tires screeching. When he got to the corner there was a blinking red light, but he didn't stop. And that's when I saw the man in the middle of the crosswalk. Next thing I knew, Jamie hit him. Then he slammed into a streetlight."

Once again, the courtroom erupted, and the judge banged more forcefully on his desk. "Order, order," he barked.

When quiet was once more restored, Cal put his hands in his pockets and rested one foot on the elevated platform where Eldon Lewis sat. "What happened then, Mr. Lewis?"

"I just kind of stood there in shock. Then Jamie got out of the car, so I knew he was okay. A couple of other cars came by a minute or two later and stopped."

"Did you report this to anyone?"

The man looked down and shook his head. "No. I—I didn't want to get involved, and other people had already stopped. So I knew someone would call the police."

"Did you realize you were the only eyewitness?"

"No. Not until you folks told me."

"Mr. Lewis, let me ask you one final question. Is there any doubt in your mind that the man you saw

on the night of September fourth was Jamie Johnson?''

''No, sir. It was him, all right.''

''Thank you, Mr. Lewis. No further questions at
this time, Your Honor, but I'd like to reserve the right
to recall this witness.''

The judge nodded. ''Does the defense wish to
question the witness?''

Jamie Johnson's lead attorney stood. It was obvious
that the testimony of Cal's witness had taken the defense team off guard, and Johnson himself was clearly
angry. ''The defense would like to request an ad-
journment until Monday so that we can process this
new information over the weekend, Your Honor.''

''Very well. We will reconvene at ten o'clock
Monday morning. Court dismissed.''

Amy instantly rose and headed toward the door,
pushing through the crowd, her cell phone in hand.
She needed to alert the station to get ready for a live
feed. Steve was waiting in front of the courthouse,
and she intended to catch Johnson on tape as he exited. She also needed to review the notes she'd taken
and organize her thoughts for her on-camera report.

Steve was off to one side of the courthouse as she
exited, and he quickly joined her.

''What gives?''

''The prosecution came up with an eyewitness.''

Steve gave a low whistle. ''Big news.''

''I think Johnson and his lawyers will come out the
front. They aren't going to be expecting any of the
TV stations to be here. I want to catch them off guard
and see if we can get a comment.''

Steve hefted the camera to his shoulder. "I'm with you."

Amy stepped to one side of the main door, her heart banging against her rib cage. She forced herself to take several long, deep breaths. Her lips and throat felt dry, and she wished she had a drink of water. But she didn't dare leave her post. Johnson could be along any minute. And, thanks to Cal, she would at last have her scoop.

By the time the pandemonium in the courtroom quieted and Cal finished conferring with his own team, Amy had disappeared. A quick, sweeping glance of the room confirmed her absence—as well as the chaos in the opposing camp. His gaze lingered for a moment on Jamie Johnson, who was one angry jock. His defense team was huddled around him, and it was clear their plans were in disarray for the moment. But Cal expected a quick recovery. They would reappear Monday with both barrels loaded, and he fully expected that they would do everything they could to discredit Eldon Lewis's testimony. Unfortunately, they might very well succeed. But he hoped that the man's sincere recount would ring true with some of the jurors, or at least plant enough doubt to stave off an acquittal on the involuntary manslaughter charge.

As Cal gathered up his papers and stuffed them into his briefcase, Bill Jackson leaned over. "I sense wrath in the opposing camp."

Cal glanced again toward the defense team. "That's putting it mildly."

"We certainly took them by surprise. I expect those guys will be putting in some long hours this weekend."

Cal gave his colleague a brief, mirthless grin. "They'll be well compensated for it."

"Too true. Say, speaking of long hours, did you notice that our favorite reporter was in the courtroom again today? Talk about a coup! She'll definitely have the scoop on this news."

"Yeah." Cal picked up his briefcase. He didn't want to discuss Amy with Bill. "And as for those long hours...see you tomorrow."

Bill made a face. "I'll be glad when this is over, if for no other reason than I'll finally have my Saturdays back."

"Until the next case comes along," Cal reminded him with a wry grin as he turned to go.

As he strode out of the courtroom, he ignored the venomous looks hurled his way by Johnson. The man was clearly holding on to his control with great effort. In fact, in the absence of his lawyers, who were almost physically restraining him, Cal suspected Johnson would be punching someone out. Probably him. His seething anger was almost palpable.

As Cal stepped into the hall, he once again glanced around for Amy, but she was nowhere in sight. He supposed she was already on her way back to the station. The story would probably be in the top slot on the six o'clock news, and time would be of the essence in putting the piece together. Though he could understand her haste, he felt oddly disappointed by her absence. Which was not a good sign. Somehow, some way, he had to figure out a way to get over the attraction he felt for her. Problem was, he didn't have a clue how to go about it.

After detouring to drop some papers off in another part of the courthouse, Cal exited by a side door, glancing toward the main entrance as he stepped outside. The sight of Amy and the cameraman who had done the filming at Saint Vincent's brought him to an abrupt stop. She must be waiting for Johnson to come out, he realized with a frown. Considering the man's black mood, that might not be wise, he realized, suddenly switching directions. He needed to warn her to be prepared for the sports star's anger.

Amy was so focused on the door that she didn't even see him approach. But as he rapidly closed the distance between them, then paused a few feet away, Cal saw a great deal. He saw the slight tremor in her hand. He saw the pulse beating frantically in the hollow of her throat. He saw the way she nervously moistened her lips. He saw her swallow convulsively and take a deep breath. Most people would never notice those subtle signs of nervousness. But he did, which only caused his frown to deepen. Since when had he become something other than "most people," he wondered? Since when had he become so attuned to her nuances?

Cal didn't know the answer to those questions. All he knew was that right now, Amy was doing something she didn't enjoy. And he suddenly recalled what she had told him that night in her apartment—that there were some parts of her job she didn't particularly like. This kind of confrontational reporting was obviously one of them. A big one.

As Cal once again started forward, the main door suddenly opened and Johnson burst through, followed by his attorneys. Amy stepped forward and held the microphone out.

"Mr. Johnson, would you like to comment on the latest development in your case?"

Startled, he stopped and turned to her, his face growing even more thunderous when he saw the camera. "What the—?" He muttered an oath and roughly knocked the microphone aside. The violence of the action made Amy momentarily lose her balance, and Johnson reached over and gripped her arm as she teetered. He stepped close, towering over her. "You are asking for big trouble, lady," he said through clenched teeth, his face only inches from hers.

She stood her ground and stared up at him defiantly. "If you don't let go of my arm, you're going to be in even bigger trouble than you already are," she said coldly.

It all happened so fast that Cal was momentarily stunned. He recovered at about the same time as Johnson's lawyers, who interceded before he could reach Amy.

"Come on, Jamie," one said placatingly as he put his hand on the man's shoulder. "Let it go. Remember what we talked about inside."

The sports star hesitated for a moment, then released Amy's arm, throwing in a shove for good measure. "Yeah. But stay out of my face, you hear me?"

he called over his shoulder as his lawyers hurried him away.

Steve lowered the camera from his shoulder and shook his head. "Man, that is one angry dude. You okay?"

Amy drew a deep breath and nodded. "Did you get all that on tape?"

Steve grinned and patted the camera. "It's recorded for posterity. Not to mention the six o'clock news."

Amy managed a shaky smile. "Great. Listen, give me two minutes to go over my notes. Then we'll do a live feed."

"Sure thing. I'll wait over on the bench."

As he ambled off, Cal watched as Amy ran the palms of her hands down her slacks and closed her eyes. Though she'd stood her ground calmly and coolly with Johnson, the encounter had clearly been traumatic for her. At least clear to him, Cal amended. Yet she'd displayed an amazing degree of calm and bravado.

Cal knew that Amy considered these kinds of assignments a proving ground, a step toward the kind of reporting she really wanted to do, but watching her now, he wasn't sure the prize was worth the price. And strangely enough, he suddenly wished he could just give her her dream so she wouldn't have to deal with people like Johnson. But he knew that the best he could do was simply let her know someone cared.

"Amy?"

His voice was gentle, but she gasped and instinctively stepped back, her body tensing into a defensive posture as her eyelids flew open.

"Cal!" Her shoulders sagged and she tried to smile. "You startled me."

"I'm sorry. I came out the side door just in time to witness your encounter with Johnson. Listen, I know you said you were okay, but are you sure?" he asked, his brow furrowed worriedly.

She drew a steadying breath. "Of course."

His gaze moved to her arm, red beneath the edge of her short-sleeved jacket, and his own anger began to simmer anew. "You have grounds for assault, you know."

She shook her head impatiently. "It's not the first time something like this has happened. If I pressed charges every time someone threw his weight around, I'd spend half my life in court. It just shakes me up for a few minutes." She frowned and glanced distractedly at her watch. "I need to get my report on tape. And I want to get back to the studio and do a little editing before airtime. It's going to be tight."

Cal nodded. "I'll let you get to work, then."

He started to turn away, but paused when she reached out and tentatively touched his arm. "Cal, I... Thanks."

He looked back at her, thrown by the electric jolt that shot through him at her simple touch. And he wasn't sure how to respond to her gratitude. He was glad she'd gotten her story. But the scene he'd just witnessed had upset him more than he cared to admit. The moment Johnson had touched her, he'd wanted to deck the guy. It wasn't an impulse he had often, and considering that she was a strong, independent woman, he wasn't sure she would appreciate the fact that he'd felt the need to "rescue" her.

But what disturbed him even more was the knowledge that this scenario wasn't a one-time occurrence. This time there'd been plenty of people around to intervene. But what about the times when she was in danger and there was no one to step in? Cal wasn't a man accustomed to fear. But the realization that Amy put herself in situations where she could get hurt—badly—made his gut twist painfully.

"Why do you do this to yourself?" he said abruptly. There was anger in his question, and bewilderment. The words—and tone—surprised him as much as they did her, judging by the startled expression on her face.

"It's part of the job," she said after a moment.

"But do you *like* doing this? Do you *like* dealing with scum like Johnson?" he persisted.

"Do you?"

He shrugged dismissively. "It's part of my job."

She just looked at him, and her silence spoke more eloquently than words.

He sighed and conceded her point with a nod. "Okay, you win. But do me a favor, will you? Make it an early night."

Again she seemed momentarily taken aback. "Why?"

He frowned. Why, indeed? Because he thought she'd been through enough today? Because she worked too hard and needed a break? Because he didn't like the fine lines of strain around her eyes?

Because he cared about her more than he should, more than was wise, more than he wanted to?

The furrows in Cal's brow deepened. There was no way he could verbalize any of that. Especially since he didn't understand how he had come to feel that way.

"Never mind," he said shortly, his fingers clenching the handle of his briefcase. "It's none of my business, anyway." And with that he turned and strode away.

Amy stared after him in confusion. Now what was that all about? First he was solicitous, then he was angry. Men! It was a good thing she *wasn't* romantically involved. She'd spend her life trying to figure the guy out instead of focusing on her career. But as she watched Cal's stiff, retreating back, she was startled to realize that maybe that wouldn't be such a bad use of her time—especially if the man was Cal Richards.

Amy took a soothing sip of tea and sighed contentedly. She had a lazy Saturday morning all to herself to bask in the glow of the coup she'd pulled off yesterday. As the other stations scrambled to piece together something for their ten o'clock news programs, Amy's coverage of yesterday's events had been picked up nationally by affiliated stations, giving both her—and the story—coast-to-coast exposure. She'd even received a call from the station vice president congratulating her for her diligence and for her comprehensive coverage of the case.

Amy took another sip of tea and stuck an English

muffin in the toaster. She *was* diligent. She'd worked hard to stay one step ahead of the competition on this story, and she'd succeeded. Yesterday's piece had done exactly what she wanted it to do. It had gotten her noticed by the right people. Thanks to Cal's tip. While she might have been in court anyway yesterday, there were days when she spent less time at the trial because of other assignments. Yesterday could very well have been one of them.

As she buttered her English muffin, she suddenly recalled Cal's question yesterday about whether she liked dealing with scum like Johnson, and a shadow crossed her face. She hadn't answered him directly. Because up until now, she hadn't really answered it for herself. Mostly because it was irrelevant. Bottom line, it didn't matter what she liked or didn't like. The station chose her assignments, and she did what she was told. And did it well.

But as she munched on the muffin, she came face-to-face with something she'd been dancing around for the past couple of years. For some reason, she couldn't avoid the question anymore, couldn't chase it away to some dark corner of her consciousness. It demanded an answer. And the answer was simple. She *hated* dealing with people like Johnson. Hated it to the very depths of her being. And then came the inevitable follow-up question, the one she'd *really* been avoiding. If she hated it so much, was the end result worth all the stress and strain?

Amy stopped chewing. Up until now, she'd always kept her gaze firmly fixed on her goal—first an anchor slot, and ultimately a network position that would let her do in-depth issues reporting, such as the coverage she'd done around the Johnson case relating to alcohol abuse or with the Saint Vincent's story. Solid, feature reporting that had the potential to create awareness about problems and change lives for the better. Those were the kinds of stories that gave her the greatest satisfaction. Because they counted for something. They made a difference. And their impact was far longer lasting than anything she would ever report about the Jamie Johnson trial.

Amy frowned. Funny. In the past, whenever she'd thought about her career, she'd always listed "celebrity status" and money as her top reasons for wanting a high-profile feature job. When had they slipped to second place? What had brought her to the realization that it was the opportunity to make a positive difference in people's lives that was *most* important to her?

Amy's gaze fell on the card that had come with Cal's flowers. It was still lying on the counter, waiting for her to make what had been an oddly difficult decision—keep or pitch? Both choices seemed to symbolize something, and she wasn't ready to deal with that yet. So she'd uncharacteristically made no decision and done nothing. She reached over and fingered the card thoughtfully. Until a few weeks ago, she was content and in control, certain about what she wanted out of life. Then along came Cal Richards, with his steadfast values, solid faith and clear priorities, to disrupt her equilibrium—both emotionally and professionally.

And yet…Amy couldn't honestly say that she was sorry they'd met. Okay, so maybe it wasn't too comfortable to reexamine her carefully crafted career plan. Maybe it wasn't too comfortable to deal with her lapsed faith. Maybe it wasn't too comfortable to think about just how long she planned to defer creating the family she ultimately wanted to have. But maybe it was time.

Amy sighed. For the last few years she'd sailed along, single-mindedly focused on one thing—making it big in broadcast journalism. She was now well on her way to achieving that goal. But meeting Cal had not only made her question that journey, it had also made her realize just how lonely it had been. Even more, it made her yearn for someone special to share it with. And different though they were, she couldn't help but wistfully wonder for one brief moment what it would be like if that special someone was Cal.

Chapter Seven

"Eldon Lewis called. He was pretty upset."

Cal gave Cynthia a distracted look, then paused beside her desk and wearily raked his fingers through his hair. It had *not* been a good Monday. "I'm not surprised."

"Was it bad?"

"Brutal. I warned him they might get rough, but I didn't expect it to take such a vicious turn."

"One of those situations where he almost felt like *he* was on trial, right?"

"Right. And it certainly didn't help our case that the judge let it go on far too long, despite our objections." The weariness in his voice was now tinged with frustration.

Cynthia eyed him sympathetically. "Listen, how about I get you some coffee?"

Cal gave her a tired grin. "Since when do you offer to fetch coffee?"

"Since you look like you're about to cave in without some."

"I don't deserve you, you know."

"Yeah, I know," Cynthia said pertly as she rose and headed toward the coffeemaker. "Just remember that when you're deciding on next year's raises for your hardworking law clerks."

Cal smiled and continued toward his office. He dropped his briefcase on the desk, then went to stare pensively out the window, his hands thrust into his pockets.

"One cup of coffee," Cynthia announced a moment later.

He turned and took it from her. "Thanks. Now get out of here. Go home to that new husband of yours."

"When are *you* going home?"

He shrugged and took a sip of the coffee. "Later."

She gave an unladylike snort and planted her hands on her hips. "Maybe it's a good thing you *don't* have a wife," she declared. "The poor woman would need to keep a picture of you on hand just to remember what you look like."

"Good night, Cynthia," Cal said dryly.

She threw up her hands. "I give up!"

"Can I count on that?"

Her face grew thoughtful. "On the other hand, maybe if you *had* a wife, you'd keep more reasonable hours."

Cal groaned. "Go home, Cynthia, before you get any more ideas."

She grinned. "Oh, I'm full of ideas." Then her

face grew more sober. "Seriously, Cal, try to get out of here before midnight."

"I'll see what I can do."

Cynthia shook her head. "You're hopeless. But even if you won't take *my* advice, I intend to take yours. Good night."

When Cynthia left, Cal walked to his desk and sank into the overstuffed chair. He felt sick about the way the defense attorney had distorted the facts to discredit his witness. And there wasn't much he could say to comfort the man. Still, he had to try. So, with a weary sigh, he reached for the phone.

The man answered on the second ring.

"Mr. Lewis? Cal Richards."

"How could they do that?" the witness burst out, clearly distraught.

"I'm sorry you had to go through that," Cal said sympathetically. "In cases like this, where the stakes are very high, the defense can sometimes play pretty dirty, as I warned you. I was hoping they wouldn't this time, but I guess we gave them too much credit."

"But I know what I saw!" the man protested.

"And I'm sure it happened exactly the way you described to the court."

"But they made me sound like—like some kind of derelict! Like I made it all up. They kept dragging up all that stuff from the past, and they twisted everything I said. It wasn't fair!"

Cal drew a deep breath. No, it wasn't. But he'd seen it happen more times than he cared to remember. And though he'd done his best to keep the cross-examination focused on the Johnson incident, objecting whenever the defense attorney brought up Eldon Lewis's past, enough information had been imparted to instill doubt about the witness's credibility in the minds of the jurors. Which had been the precise intent of the defense, of course.

"I know, Mr. Lewis. But you did your best and told the truth. All we can do is hope that the jury sees that."

The man gave a bitter laugh. "I don't think that's going to happen."

After watching the jurors' faces today, Cal didn't, either. He had hoped for more from them. But the defense team had done a masterful job of planting doubt, and there was little he could do now to change that. "You did everything you could, Mr. Lewis. That's all any of us can do. And I appreciate your cooperation. I know this wasn't easy for you."

The man sighed, and suddenly his anger evaporated. "I guess I thought I'd put the past behind me, moved on as best I could with my life. This made me realize that my mistakes will always haunt me," he said resignedly.

"You *have* moved on with your life," Cal corrected him firmly. "From every standpoint—ethical, moral, legal—the defense team should never have brought all that up. It *is* history. Remember that."

"Yeah. Well, I'll be seeing you."

The line went dead, and Cal slowly replaced the receiver. The man was clearly unconvinced, and Cal felt a deep pang of regret for the need to involve him in the trial. But he'd been their only hope. It was a chance they'd had to take in the cause of justice. He'd known that the defense team might use Lewis's past against him. The man's struggle a dozen years earlier with serious depression and a temporary drinking problem shouldn't have had any bearing on the credibility of his testimony, given the exemplary life he had led for the past ten years. But Johnson's team had positioned the facts in a way that implied that the witness was still unstable and not to be fully trusted.

It was one of those days when the injustice of the justice system weighed heavily on Cal's heart. Wearily he reached for his briefcase. Despite Cynthia's advice, it was going to be a very long night. As he spread his papers out and prepared to draft an outline of his closing remarks, he wished there was someone he could talk with about his feelings, someone who would listen to his doubts and reassure him that he had done all he could, someone who could fill the empty place in his heart and offer him understanding and support.

Suddenly an image of Amy Winter flashed through his mind, and he frowned. She'd been cropping up in his thoughts more and more lately, but so far he'd been able to convince himself that it was only because she was an attractive, appealing woman, and that his reaction was simply a normal male response to a beautiful woman. But right now he wasn't thinking about her in terms of her good looks. He was thinking of her in the context of confidante/friend/comforter, he realized, his frown deepening. That was serious stuff. And it wasn't good. He wasn't in the market for romance—particularly with her, he reminded himself firmly.

Nevertheless, a surge of longing just to hear her voice swept over him, so strong that it made him catch his breath. So strong that it scared him. So strong that it made him wonder if perhaps he should give up the fight and simply let the attraction he felt for her play out, see if their differences were really as irreconcilable as they seemed.

And then logic kicked in. He had issues of his own to resolve before he even *considered* trying to deal with the issues between them. That had to be his top priority.

But first he had a closing argument to write.

"Not guilty."

A muscle twitched in Cal's jaw and his lips settled into a thin line as he stared at the judge, oblivious to the sudden pandemonium in the courtroom. It wasn't as if the verdict was a surprise. He'd known from the beginning that the odds were stacked against them. But as always, he'd held on to a sliver of hope that in the end justice would triumph. A hope that far too often was in vain.

He drew a slow, deep breath, then glanced toward Jamie Johnson. The defendant was beaming and shaking hands with his attorneys, his "golden boy" image restored. For a moment Cal actually felt sick. How could the man feel so little remorse for the life he'd carelessly destroyed? Cal hoped that at least Johnson had learned something from the experience. But he doubted it. The sports jock would probably emerge from the trial even cockier, more convinced than ever that he was invincible, he thought with a disheartened sigh.

Cal felt a hand on his shoulder and looked up.

"You did your best, you know," Bill Jackson said.

Cal gave a noncommittal shrug. "Too bad it wasn't good enough."

His colleague glanced at Johnson's legal team. "Considering the guns we were up against—not to mention the money, the sympathetic press and Johnson's boy-next-door image—don't be too hard on yourself."

Cal drew a deep breath and stood up. "Who said life was fair, right?"

"Right."

Cal held out his hand. "Well, I know one thing. I couldn't have done even half as well without you, Bill. I may have been the lead on this case, but you worked just as hard as I did. Thank you."

His colleague took his hand but brushed the comment aside. "You've done the same for me in the past. And will again, no doubt."

Cal smiled. "Count on it."

"See you back at the office?"

"Yeah. I'll be along in a few minutes."

By the time Cal packed up his papers and left, the courtroom was mostly empty. He strode down the hall toward the front entrance of the building, then suddenly changed his mind and veered off toward a side door. No doubt Johnson was triumphantly holding court for a gaggle of reporters, and that was one show he had no desire to see. He assumed Amy was among them. What had been her reaction to the outcome? he

Get 2 Books FREE!

Steeple Hill®
publisher of inspirational Christian fiction, presents

Love Inspired®

a new series of contemporary love stories that will lift your spirits and reinforce important lessons about life, faith and love!

FREE BOOKS!
Get two free books by best-selling Christian authors!

FREE GIFT!
Get an exciting mystery gift absolutely free!

2 FREE BOOKS!

▲ To get your 2 free books and a free gift, affix this peel-off sticker to the reply card and mail it today!

Love Inspired®

Get 2

HOW TO GET YOUR
2 FREE BOOKS AND FREE GIFT

1. Peel off the 2 FREE BOOKS seal from the front cover. Place it in the space provided at right. This automatically entitles you to receive two free books and an exciting mystery gift.

2. Send back this card and you'll get 2 Love Inspired® novels. These books have a combined cover price of $9.00 in the U.S. and $10.50 in Canada, but they are yours to keep absolutely FREE!

3. There's <u>no</u> catch. You're under <u>no</u> obligation to buy anything. We charge nothing – ZERO – for your first shipment. And you don't have to make any minimum number of purchases – not even one!

4. We call this line Love Inspired because each month you'll receive novels that are filled with joy, faith and true Christian values. The stories will lift your spirits and gladden your heart! You'll like the convenience of getting them delivered to your home well before they are in stores. And you'll like our discount prices too!

5. We hope that after receiving your free books you'll want to remain a subscriber. But the choice is yours – to continue or cancel, anytime at all! So why not take us up on our invitation, with no risk of any kind. You'll be glad you did!

6. And remember...we'll send you a mystery gift ABSOLUTELY FREE just for giving Love Inspired a try!

Steeple Hill®

SPECIAL FREE GIFT!

We'll send you a fabulous mystery gift, absolutely FREE, simply for accepting our no-risk offer!

Books FREE!

HURRY! Return this card promptly to get 2 FREE books and a FREE gift!

Love Inspired®

YES, send me the 2 FREE *Love Inspired* novels and FREE gift, as explained on the back. I understand that I am under no obligation to purchase anything further.

Affix peel-off 2 FREE BOOKS sticker here.

NAME (PLEASE PRINT CLEARLY)

ADDRESS

APT.# CITY

STATE/PROV. ZIP/POSTAL CODE

303 IDL CQEK

103 IDL CQEL
(LI-LA-01/00)

Steeple Hill Reader Service™—Here's How it Works:

Accepting your 2 free books and gift places you under no obligation to buy anything. You may keep the books and gift and return the shipping statement marked "cancel." If you do not cancel, about a month later we will send you 3 additional novels and bill you just $3.74 each in the U.S., or $3.96 each in Canada, plus 25¢ delivery per book and applicable taxes if any.* That's the complete price, and — compared to cover prices of $4.50 in the U.S. and $5.25 in Canada — quite a bargain! You may cancel at any time, but if you choose to continue, every month we'll send you 3 more books, which you may either purchase at the discount price...or return to us and cancel your subscription.

*Terms and prices subject to change without notice. Sales tax applicable in N.Y.
Canadian residents will be charged applicable provincial taxes and GST.

BUSINESS REPLY MAIL
FIRST-CLASS MAIL   PERMIT NO. 717   BUFFALO NY

POSTAGE WILL BE PAID BY ADDRESSEE

STEEPLE HILL READER SERVICE
3010 WALDEN AVE
PO BOX 1867
BUFFALO NY 14240-9952

NO POSTAGE
NECESSARY
IF MAILED
IN THE
UNITED STATES

If offer card is missing write to: Steeple Hill Reader Service, 3010 Walden Ave., P.O. Box 1867, Buffalo, NY 14240-1867 wondered. Surprise? Anger? Disappointment—in him?

The last question gnawed at him. He tried to tell himself that it didn't matter, but in his heart he knew it did. Because like it or not, he cared what she thought about him.

And he had his answer a few minutes later when he reached his office and discovered on his voice mail the slightly husky voice he found so appealing.

"Cal. Amy. I wanted to let you know how sorry I am about the verdict. You did everything humanly possible to convict Johnson, and I thought your entire prosecution—especially your closing argument—was masterful. How the jury could let that scumbag off is beyond me. I would have waited to talk with you, but I had to file the story and you were pretty tied up, so this is the best I could do." There was a moment of silence, and when she spoke again her voice had taken on a different, more personal—and slightly uncertain—tone. "Listen, I don't suppose our paths are likely to cross again anytime soon, so I just wanted to say that I... Well, it's been a privilege to get to know you. I really enjoyed the time we spent together. And I wanted to wish you all the best in the future."

The line went dead, and Cal slowly replaced the receiver. He knew she was working at warp speed to get the story ready for the evening news, and he was touched that she had taken time to place the call. He hadn't expected it. Or even let himself *hope* for it. Just as he hadn't allowed himself to dwell on the fact that she would no longer be a daily—albeit professional—presence in his life. Though they had rarely spoken, merely knowing she was in the courtroom had brightened his days. Now he had to face the fact that even that limited contact had come to an end. It left him feeling strangely empty—and more than a little melancholy.

"You've been summoned by the chief, Cal."

Cynthia's voice intruded on his thoughts and Cal glanced at her, forcing himself to shift gears. "Okay. I'm on my way."

As he strode down the hall to David Morgan's office, he wondered what the senior member of the department would say about the outcome of the case. He hoped Morgan wasn't disappointed in his performance. Cal, like all of the staff attorneys, had great respect for the older man's opinion. His incisive legal mind, combined with a great sense of fairness and humanitarianism, had made him almost a legend in the Atlanta legal community. His praise—or censure—was never taken lightly.

Morgan's secretary glanced up when he entered, then waved him inside. "He's expecting you."

The older man was engrossed in something on his computer screen, but he looked up immediately when Cal stepped to the door and knocked lightly.

"Come in, Cal. Have a seat. Would you like something to drink?"

"How about a gin and tonic?" Cal replied with a wry grin. At the older man's startled look, he added a quick disclaimer. "Just kidding," he assured him.

"For a minute I wondered if the trial might have been even more stressful than I thought," Morgan said with relief. "I've never known you to drink anything more than an occasional glass of wine."

"I still don't."

"Well, you probably *could* use something stronger after these last few months. I know how hard you worked on the Johnson case. And I know how hard it is to lose. I've been there. Feel like doing a little rehashing?"

Cal nodded. "Sure."

"Tell me about the approach the defense used."

By the time Cal talked the case through with the older man, recounting the defense's tactics and his strategy, he felt a lot better about the decisions he'd made in planning his prosecution. And he suspected that had been Morgan's intent.

"So I'm not happy with the verdict, but I honestly don't know what I would have done differently," Cal concluded, feeling more at peace with the outcome.

Morgan nodded. "Your approach was sound. By rights, you should have won. But a lot of factors that we have no control over often influence the outcome. That's what happened here, you know."

"I'm beginning to accept that."

"Good. I don't want you beating yourself up over this. You're a fine attorney, and you did as much as anyone could have in this case. More, I'd venture to say."

Cal felt a flush of pleasure at the older man's praise. "Thank you."

"So now I want you to take a few days off. Can't have our people working themselves into the ground."

Cal hesitated. "Actually, I was saving my vacation for later in the summer."

The older man waved his protest aside. "Who said anything about vacation? How many hours a week have you put in for this trial? How many weekends have you worked?"

"A few," Cal acknowledged.

Morgan snorted. "That's an understatement if I ever heard one. Just go, boy. Spend a few days in those mountains you love. Although why I send you there, I don't know. I have a feeling one of these days you won't come back." He eyed the younger man shrewdly.

Cal shifted uncomfortably. "I'll be back," he promised.

"This time," the older man amended. "But what about next time? None of my business, of course. But I want you to know that you have a bright future here."

"I appreciate that."

"Just stating the facts, son. Now go tie up the loose ends of this case and take off for a few days."

"Thank you, sir."

"No need to thank me. You earned it."

Yes, he had, Cal acknowledged as he made his way back to his office. It had been a grueling few months. All trials were stressful, but the high-profile nature of this case had increased the pressure exponentially. Though the trial itself had been relatively brief, the months of behind-the-scenes research and preparation had taken a toll, and he was tired. He needed a break. Except for brief visits home on major holidays, he hadn't had more than two consecutive days off in almost a year.

Home. The word itself was telling, he mused. That was how he thought of the mountains. And Morgan, with his keen insight, had picked up on that. Perhaps on this trip he would find a way to talk to his father about his growing desire to return, Cal reflected. He would find a way to make Jack Richards understand that his definition of success wasn't necessarily his son's. The last thing in the world Cal wanted to do was disappoint the man who had given so selflessly to him for so many years. But he had to live his own life. And he was growing more and more certain that he wanted to live it in the mountains.

Amy glanced at the phone for the tenth time in as many minutes. She hadn't heard from Cal since she left the message for him earlier in the week, but then, why should she? she told herself curtly. He had no reason to call her. Sure, they'd spent a couple of pleasant evenings together. But neither one had been a "real" date. The first night she'd *bought* his time. And the dinner at Rick's resulted from a chance meeting at Saint Vincent's. The few words they'd subsequently exchanged during the trial hardly counted as "social" interaction. There was certainly nothing in any of their encounters on which to base a relationship. Which she didn't want, anyway, of course—right?

Amy sat back in her desk chair and sighed. Six weeks ago—was it only six weeks?—she would have answered that question with a resounding "Right!"

She'd been perfectly happy with her life. She'd known exactly what she wanted and exactly how she intended to go about getting it. Relationships weren't even *on* her list of priorities. She considered them a distraction, an impediment to her career goals. And career was everything.

But that was BC—before Cal. Somehow, her BC life now seemed shallow and empty. The goals she'd prized so highly—fame, power, prestige, money—no longer had quite the same luster or appeal. Instead, she'd come to discover that the work itself was just as important to her. Especially issue-oriented kinds of stories. But only since Cal entered her life had she begun to analyze *why*.

It was becoming more and more clear to her that despite her efforts to leave her farm roots behind, to live the life of big-city glitz and glamour, at heart she was still the same Amy Ann Winter who had been raised in a loving family with solid values and instilled with a belief that she should count among her priorities a commitment to doing good work that made life better for other people. She was still the same young girl who had been brought up to believe that the real satisfaction in life came from focusing on others, not on oneself. It was part of who she was. Period.

She'd pushed that upbringing aside for seven years as she devoted herself to making her mark in broadcast journalism. And she was succeeding. But at what price? Though she'd learned to play them, she didn't like the political games. She didn't like the jockeying for power. She didn't like the cutthroat nature of a business in which you had rivals, not friends. And she especially didn't like dealing with the Jamie Johnsons of the world.

At the same time, she was good at what she did. She not only had a solid news sense, but even better, a knack for ferreting out the "story behind the story." That skill had brought her to the attention of the "right" people more than once. They had recognized that her coverage was more thorough, well-rounded and dimensional than that of her competitors, and that was gratifying. But she now knew that covering fast-breaking stories just didn't cut it for her, good as she was at it. She was ready to move on to pure feature work, work that had a lasting impact on people's lives. It was time.

There was only one little problem, she thought with a sigh. Because she *was* so good at what she currently did, more and more of these assignments were coming her way. While she'd worked hard to put some meat on her coverage of the Jamie Johnson case, for most of the stations the story had been more about entertainment than reporting. It certainly hadn't been about justice. No wonder Cal had such a poor opinion of the press.

Amy propped her chin in her hand. A few weeks ago, if someone had told her that she'd feel sympathetic toward Cal Richards she would have laughed in their face. And the notion that she would actually *like* him would have been ludicrous. Though they were different in many ways, she admired Cal. He had impeccable ethics built on a solid foundation of faith; he was generous and kind; and he radiated strength and trustworthiness. Bottom line, he was the kind of person she would like to have as a friend.

The phone rang, startling her out of her reverie. She wondered—as she had every time it had rung since she'd left her message—if Cal might be on the other end, and the thought sent her pulse into double time. Yet a phone call from someone toward whom she felt merely "friendly" would hardly produce such a visceral response, she realized with a startled frown before a second ring prompted her to pick up the receiver.

"Amy? We've got a hostage situation at a day-care center. We need you there pronto. Steve is already on the way."

Amy automatically switched gears and reached for a notepad. But even as she jotted down the information the news editor was relaying, she acknowledged that she'd been dodging her feelings about Cal for too long. It was time to face them and either put the relationship to rest—or do something about exploring it. Though she'd always considered relationships too much of a distraction, Cal Richards was proving to be a distraction with or without a relationship, she admitted. And until she figured out how—or if—he fit into her life, she didn't think that was going to change.

Cal folded his long frame into his favorite overstuffed chair, opened a can of soda, picked up the newspaper and punched the remote on the television. This was the first night in weeks that he'd been home in time to watch the evening news on his own TV, and he intended to savor every moment. Now that the burden of the trial was lifted from his shoulders, he felt more relaxed than he had in months.

He settled back and glanced at the screen. He wasn't particularly interested in the events of the day, but he *was* interested in seeing Amy. In the past couple of days he'd been tempted to call her more times than he cared to admit, but so far he'd resisted. He needed to get his life in order first, and he hoped the trip home would help him do that. In fact, in forty-eight hours he'd be sitting down to some of Gram's homemade biscuits and gravy right about now. He could hardly wait, he thought with a grin.

Cal scanned the newspaper, giving only marginal attention to the TV until the news program began and he discovered that Amy was covering the lead story.

"The Child First Day-Care Center is the scene of a drama that began this afternoon at three when a gunman entered the facility and took the students and teachers in one of the classrooms hostage," announced the anchorman. "He has been tentatively identified as the father of a former student who died in a bus crash on one of the school's field trips. We go live now to reporter Amy Winter who is on the scene. Amy, can you give us an update on the situation?"

A shot of Amy standing across the street from the day-care facility filled the screen.

"It now appears that there may also be a bomb involved, Peter. A few moments ago the gunman issued a warning that if police try to enter the building he will, and I quote, 'blow the place up.' He has also been positively identified as Roger Wilson, whose son, Dennis, was killed about a year ago in the bus accident you mentioned. Following that incident, Mr. Wilson unsuccessfully sued the center for negligence. According to his ex-wife, whom I spoke with moments ago by phone, he has been under psychiatric care for some time and may have a drug problem.''

''How many hostages are still inside?'' the anchorman asked.

''Eight children, ages three and four, and two teachers. The gunman has yet to make any demands, so at this point the authorities are waiting to—''

An explosion suddenly ripped through the air, and the camera jerked, making the image of Amy tilt crazily. Cal jumped to his feet, nearly choking on the soda he'd just swallowed. Pandemonium broke out at the scene, and the camera showed media and bystanders ducking for cover before it refocused on the day-care center.

''Peter, as you can see, the bomb threat wasn't an idle one.'' Though Amy's voice was controlled, the slight quiver that ran through it told Cal she was badly shaken. But she was all right, thank God! ''It appears that the explosion occurred at the rear of the building, which is relatively close to where the hostages are....''

Suddenly a toddler appeared at the front door of the day-care center, and Amy paused and turned as a murmur ran through the crowd. The little boy was clearly dazed, and there was blood on his face. A hush fell over the scene as he wobbled unsteadily into the open, then faltered, and Cal heard Amy whisper, "Dear God!"

The child stood there for several eternal seconds as the bystanders stared at him in shock. Just as Cal thought, Why doesn't someone do something? Amy suddenly appeared in front of the camera. Cal caught his breath sharply as she slipped through the police barricade, dashed toward the toddler and scooped him up, cradling him protectively against her chest. She turned and started to run back toward the camera, but she'd only gone a couple of steps when a second explosion ripped through the building. This one was much closer to the front and spewed debris in all directions. Amy staggered momentarily, then continued her flight. The camera stayed on her as she returned to the safety of the sidelines and gently placed the crying child in the waiting arms of a paramedic. Someone thrust a microphone into her hands, and she stared down at it in confusion.

Suddenly a paramedic touched her shoulder. "Ma'am, I think you're hurt. Why don't you let me take a look?"

Amy turned. The back of her hair was matted with blood, and Cal felt like someone had kicked him in the gut. Suddenly she swayed, and as he watched in horror, her face took on an ashen tone and she crumpled to the ground.

And then the live feed went dead.

Chapter Eight

Cal's heart stopped, then lurched on, and his hand convulsively crushed the soda can. Every nerve in his body was taut and his lungs seem paralyzed as he stared at the screen.

The scene shifted back to the studio. "We'll keep you informed about the situation at First Child Day-Care Center just as soon as we have additional information," the anchorman promised.

The co-anchor started talking about some sort of labor contract that had been signed that day, and Cal stared at her incredulously. How in heaven's name could they go on with the news as if nothing had happened? *Didn't they realize that Amy could be seriously injured?*

Throughout his career, Cal had scrupulously avoided using his connections for personal reasons. But during the next five minutes he used every one he could muster. And after several terse calls, he had the information he wanted.

* * *

Amy stared up groggily at the nurse, trying vainly to focus on her face. From her curled-up fetal position, she was looking at the woman sideways, which didn't help in the least.

"There's someone here who would like to see you," the woman said in a voice that seemed to come from far away. "He's been waiting for quite some time. May I let him come in?"

Amy blinked, still trying to clear her vision. But the effort only made her head hurt worse. "Who is it?" she mumbled.

"He didn't give his name. He just said he was a close friend."

Amy frowned, trying to concentrate. It must be Steve, though she was surprised he hadn't stayed at the scene to continue his live coverage. After all, it was a hot story. But who else could it be?

"Okay," she agreed, closing her eyes against the bright lights. The nurse's shoes squeaked on the tile floor as she retreated, and Amy felt herself quickly drifting back into oblivion. She didn't fight the blackness. Maybe the next time she woke up, her head wouldn't hurt so much and—

"I hope you don't mind if I stretched the truth a bit to get in here."

The familiar, though slightly roughened, voice brought her abruptly back to reality, and her eyelids flew open. She squinted against the lights as she stared up at the tall, slightly out-of-focus figure towering above her. "Cal?"

"Yeah. It's me."

She made an attempt to sit up, but he restrained her with a gentle but firm hand on her shoulder. She heard the sound of a chair being pulled across the floor, and then he sat beside her, his face only inches from hers.

"I don't think you're supposed to move around too much," he said gently. "I'll come down to your level, okay?"

Amy continued to stare at him incredulously. Never in a million years would she have expected Cal to show up at the hospital. But she had never been happier to see anyone in her life, she realized with a start. Suddenly her throat constricted and she found herself close to tears. Without even stopping to consider, she reached out a hand and drew a deep, shuddering breath. "Oh, Cal." It was all she could manage.

He enfolded her hand in a warm, firm clasp. "It's okay, Amy," he said with an odd catch in his voice. "It's over. You'll be fine."

The words were as much to reassure himself as her, he realized, as he studied her pale face and tried to swallow past the lump in his throat. He was still badly shaken by his first sight of her, huddled under the thin white blanket on the gurney, looking so fragile and vulnerable—the antithesis of the strong, gutsy woman he had come to know. And he didn't feel much more reassured up close. Her luminous green eyes were slightly dazed, and in her hand he could feel the tremors that still radiated throughout her body.

Cal watched as she closed her eyes and struggled to keep her tears in check, the spiky fan of her damp, dark lashes sweeping against her too-pale cheeks. He wanted to tell her not to bother, to go ahead and cry. But she was a woman accustomed to being in charge, and he understood her need to regain some semblance of control. So he waited quietly, simply stroking his thumb comfortingly over the back of her hand.

As Amy struggled to stem the tears that threatened to spill from her eyes, she tried to come to grips with Cal's presence. Why had he come? What did it mean? She hadn't heard from him since the trial ended, had come to the conclusion that any further contact between them would have to be initiated by her. She hadn't figured out just what she was going to do about that—if anything. But now fate had dramatically stepped in, taking the decision out of her hands. Cal was here, and she was happy.

Amy knew that those last two facts were significant, and that she'd have to think about them later. But right now her brain felt too fuzzy to process anything other than gratitude.

When she at last felt more in control of her emotions, she drew a long, shaky breath and opened her eyes. Cal's face was still only inches away, and at this proximity, she noticed things she'd never seen before. The irises of his troubled, deep brown eyes were flecked with gold, for example, and there was a fine sprinkling of gray at his temples. The two deeply etched lines in his brow made her yearn to reach over and smooth them away, but she resisted the impulse, letting her gaze drop to his lips instead. They were set in a grim, unsmiling line, and his jaw was rigid with tension. The strain of the last few hours was clearly evident in his haggard face—and all because of her, she marveled, deeply touched by his concern but also sorry to be the cause of it.

"Please don't worry," she murmured.

He squeezed her hand, and forced his lips into a smile. "Well, it's not every day I see someone I—" He paused and cleared his throat. "Someone I know practically get blown up on TV."

He tried for a light tone, but he was shaken by what he'd almost said to Amy. Fortunately, she didn't seem to notice.

The door opened, and they both glanced toward the white-coated figure who entered. The woman looked at Amy as she approached them, then held out her hand to Cal.

"I'm Dr. Whitney. And you're...?"

"Cal Richards. I'm a friend of Amy's."

The woman nodded, then turned her attention to Amy. "I've checked the X rays, Ms. Winter. You're one lucky lady. Everything looks fine. There isn't even any evidence of a concussion."

Amy managed a weak grin. "My mother always said I had a hard head."

"Not too hard," the doctor amended. "The flying debris put a nice gouge in the back. To the tune of twenty stitches, in fact. Fortunately, once your hair grows back, you'll never notice the scar."

"How about the little boy, doctor? And the others in the building?"

"A number were injured in the explosions, but there were no fatalities. Thanks to you, the boy has just minor cuts and abrasions. But it would be a different story if he'd still been standing by the building when the second explosion went off.''

Amy shrugged dismissively. ''Someone else would have gone to get him if I hadn't.''

Cal's hand tightened around hers, and she was struck by the intensity in his eyes when she looked up at him. ''But everyone else hesitated, Amy. You didn't.''

''He's right,'' the doctor confirmed.

Amy tore her gaze away from Cal's. ''I love kids. It was just instinctive.''

The doctor glanced at Cal. ''This is one special lady, you know.''

Cal nodded. ''Yeah. I know.''

''Okay, here's the scoop,'' the doctor continued, turning her attention back to Amy. ''We have no reason to keep you. You'll probably recover much faster at home, anyway. I'll give you a prescription for pain, but the best thing you can do for the next few days is rest. You may experience a bit of light-headedness for the next day or two, so move slowly. You can see your own doctor to have the stitches removed in a few days. Any questions?''

''No.''

''Let's have you sit up, then.''

The woman reached over to assist Amy, and Cal moved to her other side. She carefully swung her legs over the edge of the gurney and let them dangle for a moment, closing her eyes as a wave of dizziness and nausea swept over her.

''Oh, wow,'' Amy said faintly, gripping the edge

of the gurney. She felt Cal move closer and put his arm around her shoulder.

"Dizzy?" the doctor asked.

She nodded.

"Nauseous?"

Again Amy nodded.

"Just sit there a moment and breathe steadily. It should pass quickly."

Amy kept her eyes closed and focused on following the doctor's instructions. When she finally felt more normal, she opened her eyes.

"Okay?" the doctor asked, studying her critically.

"I think so."

"Your blouse and jacket are on the chair," the woman said, nodding toward the items. "Can you manage, or should I send a nurse in?"

Amy's head was rapidly clearing, and she shook her head. "No. I can handle it."

The doctor glanced at Cal. "Will you see that she gets home? Or should we call someone else?"

"I'll take her."

"Good. All right, Ms. Winter. You should be fine. If you have any problems—extended dizziness, excessive bleeding from the cut—let us know. You'll need to change the dressing every day, maybe twice a day for the first couple of days. I'll have a nurse bring in some gauze and tape for you, along with the prescription."

"Thank you."

"My pleasure," the woman said with a smile. "We don't get too many heroes in here."

Amy flushed, then turned to Cal as the woman exited. He was looking at her with such tenderness that her breath caught in her throat. If she didn't know better… But no, that was ridiculous. That knock on the head was giving her all sorts of crazy ideas. Besides, his expression was gone so quickly that she wondered if she'd just imagined it.

"Ready to go home?"

She nodded. "Could you hand me my clothes?"

"Can you manage this?" he asked as he retrieved her blouse and jacket.

"I think so." She reached around, then frowned. "Except maybe for the ties on this gown. Would you undo them?"

"Sure." He stepped to her side and she angled her body away from him. The green hospital gown was tied in two places, and as his fingers worked the knots he tried to ignore the expanse of creamy skin visible between the edges of the gown. It wasn't easy. More than once his fingers inadvertently brushed against the curve of her slender back, and each time an electric shock seemed to ricochet through him, jolting him not only physically, but emotionally. No other woman had ever drawn such a powerful response from him with so little provocation. That response, coming on the heels of his unexpectedly gut-wrenching panic at her injury, left him floundering in an unfamiliar sea of emotions.

He fumbled through the second tie, drawing a ragged breath when at last it slipped open. "Should I leave while you change?" he asked unsteadily.

She shook her head. "Just turn around, please."

Cal gladly complied. He needed some time to compose himself and get off the emotional roller coaster he was on. Like a couple of weeks, maybe. Unfortunately, the two minutes it took Amy to change wasn't nearly enough.

"Okay. I'm decent."

He turned slowly, and though she smiled, he could see the weariness and pain in her face.

"I'd be happy to call a cab, Cal," she offered. "I hate to put you to all this trouble."

"Forget it."

From the tone of his voice, she figured the subject wasn't open to discussion. And she wasn't up to one, anyway. Instead, she gripped the edge of the gurney and started to stand.

Cal was beside her in an instant. "Whoa! Remember what the doctor said. Move slowly." He put an arm around her shoulders. "Okay, try it now."

Amy rose gingerly to her feet. She swayed for a moment, and he gave her a worried look as he tightened his grip.

"I'm okay," she assured him. "Just a little light-headed."

Before he could reply, a knock at the door drew their attention, and the nurse entered. "Dr. Whitney said to give you these." She held out a package of gauze and a prescription, and Cal took them. "Do you need any help getting to your car? Would you like a wheelchair?"

"Yes."

"No."

They spoke simultaneously, and Amy glanced up at Cal. "I can walk."

For a moment she thought he was going to argue, but instead he turned to the nurse. "Could you wait with her at the entrance while I pull up?"

"No problem."

"That's really not necessary," Amy protested.

"Humor me, okay?"

There was something intense but unreadable in his eyes that made Amy's protest die in her throat. "Okay."

By the time she was safely buckled into his car a few minutes later and they were on their way, a deep-seated weariness had settled over her. She answered his few questions in monosyllables, and was grateful when he lapsed into silence. Though the drive home was swift, with just one stop to get her prescription filled, the road seemed excessively bumpy, and the throbbing pain in her head intensified. When they at last pulled into her parking lot she let out an audible sigh of relief.

Cal parked the car and glanced over at her with a worried frown. He'd been stealing looks at her throughout the drive, and she seemed to have grown paler over the past half hour. He wasn't entirely convinced that the hospital should have released her, but he supposed the doctor was right. She would get more rest here.

"Wait there. I'll come around and help you out," he instructed.

Amy acquiesced with a nod. She'd planned to simply thank Cal in the parking lot and send him on his way, but she suddenly felt too shaky to make it into her apartment without help.

"Okay, nice and easy," he said as he pulled her door open and extended his hand.

With his help, she stood carefully—only to suddenly find herself in his arms.

"Just take a minute to get your sea legs," he said huskily as he held her protectively against his chest. He had planned to give her a moment to get her balance—but he lost his the second her soft curves pressed against the length of his body. She felt so good in his arms. So right. A powerful surge of yearning swept over him, and it took every ounce of his willpower to fight the temptation to lean down and taste the sweetness of her lips.

Cal swallowed convulsively. He didn't want to feel this way about Amy. And he especially didn't want to feel this way right now, when he was struggling with other choices and decisions that would affect the rest of his life. Cal didn't understand why the Lord had put this woman in his life at this particular time, but he also trusted that there must be a reason. And so he turned to the Master, as he often did in times of turmoil, for guidance.

Dear Lord, I'm confused, he prayed as he held Amy in his arms. *After today, I know that I care deeply about this woman. But we seem ill suited in so many ways. Our priorities—and our lifestyles—are completely different. Amy could never be happy in a cabin in the mountains. But I'm more and more convinced that I can't be happy anywhere else. Please, Lord, help me resolve this dilemma and give me the wisdom to discern Your will.*

As Amy leaned against Cal, savoring the haven of

his strong, sure arms, she felt strangely content. She wasn't a woman who leaned on *anyone* very often, but at this moment it felt wonderful. In fact, oddly enough, it felt as if she'd somehow come home. She didn't understand the feeling, but neither did she fight it. It felt too good. So with a sigh, she closed her eyes and nestled her cheek against his chest, conscious of the rapid beat of his heart beneath her ear. Amy didn't think his elevated pulse was from the exertion of helping her out of the car, and a sudden tingle of excitement ran through her that had nothing to do with her recent trauma.

Cal felt her tremble and pulled back slightly to gaze down at her, his eyes troubled. "Are you okay?"

No, she wasn't. Her own pulse had gone haywire, and she was having trouble breathing as she grappled with her own conflicting emotions. It felt way too good in this man's arms. And though she tried desperately to stifle the thought, she couldn't stop wondering what it would be like to feel his lips on hers.

"Amy?"

Cal's worried voice brought her back to reality, and she forced her stiff lips into the semblance of a smile. "I'll be better once I'm inside."

If Cal noticed the unevenness in her voice, he made no comment. Instead, he closed the door and took her arm, matching his pace to hers as she made her way slowly to the door. She fumbled in her purse, all too conscious of his hand resting protectively in the small of her back. When her fingers closed over the key, she turned to him and again summoned up a smile.

"Thank you for everything, Cal. I'm really sorry

about tonight. I'm sure you had better plans for your evening then spending it at the hospital."

He tilted his head and gave her a crooked grin. "Are you telling me to get lost?"

She looked at him in surprise. "Of course not. You're welcome to come in. I just don't want to ruin the rest of your evening."

He reached over and took the key from her hand. "Trust me, Amy. This is where I want to be."

She didn't know how to respond to that, so she simply let him open the door and guide her inside.

"Why don't you sit down and I'll get you some water so you can take a pill?"

"You really don't have to wait on me, you know. I'm used to taking care of myself."

He turned toward her and placed both hands lightly on her shoulders. "I know. You're a very strong, independent woman. But you've had one tough day. And frankly, so have I. It's not a pretty thing to watch someone you—you care about get hurt right in front of your eyes. In fact, it's as close to hell as I ever want to get. So let me do this for you, okay? It will make me feel better."

Cal had a way of making it sound like *he* was the beneficiary of his own good deeds, Amy realized, remembering his comment about his work at Saint Vincent's. And positioned that way, she could hardly object.

"You win," she capitulated.

When he returned a few moments later, she was playing back the messages on her answering machine.

"I need to call the news editor back. The rest can wait," she told him.

He handed her the water and a pill. "Would you like some dinner?"

She made a face. "No way. I'm still kind of queasy. What time is it, anyway?" She glanced at her watch and her eyes widened. "Ten o'clock! I must have been at the hospital for hours. What about you? Did you have dinner?"

"Not yet."

"Oh, Cal! You must be starving!"

"Only in the last few minutes."

"I've got some microwave stuff in the freezer. You're welcome to anything in there, but I think my supply is pretty depleted," she said apologetically.

He grinned. "A starving man isn't very picky. Go ahead and make your call while I scrounge something up."

The news editor wasn't available, but the station promised to have him get back to her shortly. She rose to go to the bathroom, pausing in the kitchen doorway to find Cal with a chocolate-chip cookie stuck in his mouth as he searched through her freezer.

"That's not very nutritious," she teased.

He turned to her and removed the cookie. "Maybe not. But it's very available."

"True," she conceded. "Listen, would you mind answering the phone while I change into something more casual? My station should be calling back any minute."

"Sure. Take your time."

Amy continued to the bathroom, where she washed

her face and then used a hand mirror to gingerly examine the back of her head in the vanity mirror, cringing when she saw the large white bandage. Good thing they only showed her from the front on camera, she thought wryly. It was going to take a long time for all that hair to grow back.

Just as she finished dressing she heard the phone ring, and she padded barefoot toward the living room, tucking her T-shirt into her sweatpants as she walked.

"Yes, she's okay," she heard Cal say. "Shaken up, of course, and she has a nasty cut on the back of her head. But the doctor said she'll be fine."

There was a moment of silence, then he spoke again.

"No, don't worry. I'm going to stay tonight until she's settled. And I'll stop by to check on her again first thing in the morning…Mmm-hmm…I already asked, but she said no. Any suggestions on what might whet her appetite in the morning if she's still not hungry?"

Amy's brows rose in surprise and she paused in the doorway. Jarrod Blake, the night news editor, was good at his job, but it wasn't like him to ask about anyone's health—or eating habits—in any detail. And he certainly wouldn't know anything about Amy's favorite foods.

Cal listened for a moment, then turned and caught sight of her. "She just walked in. I'll put her on." He covered the mouthpiece with his hand. "Your sister," he said.

Amy frowned and walked toward him. "Kate?"

"She saw your clip on the national news a few

minutes ago, and she sounded pretty frantic. I told her you were okay, but I don't think she'll believe it until she hears your voice."

Amy reached for the phone. "Kate?"

"Oh, Amy! I was so afraid you were—" Her voice broke on a strangled sob.

"Kate, really, it's okay," Amy reassured her. She gently lowered herself into the desk chair, her gaze on Cal's broad back as retreated to the kitchen. "I just needed a few stitches."

"I wish I could be there with you!"

"I love you for the thought, but really, I'm okay. Cal is here. And you've got that baby to think about. Please, don't worry."

"Have you heard from Mom?"

"No. Have you? Did she see it, too?" Amy asked in alarm.

"I guess not, or she would have called. But she'll hear about it in the morning from someone."

"I'll call her first thing," Amy promised.

"Okay." Kate was beginning to sound more like herself. "Listen, isn't this Cal the one you bought the date with at that auction?"

"Yeah."

"I didn't know you'd been seeing him."

"I haven't been."

"Then what's he doing there?"

Amy lowered her voice. "I don't know. He just showed up at the hospital, and then he brought me home."

"I thought you said there wasn't anything between you two?"

"I didn't think there was."

"Hmm. Sounds like you better revise your thinking, sister dear."

"What I think is that you're reading too much into this," Amy said firmly. "Besides, my head hurts too much to think about this tonight."

"You're right," Kate said, instantly contrite. "Go to bed and get some rest. Will you call me tomorrow and let me know how you are?"

"Of course."

"Say good-night to Cal for me. And, Amy…he sounds really nice."

As Amy rang off, she couldn't disagree with Kate's assessment. Especially when Cal walked in a moment later bearing a plate of toast and a cup of tea.

"I know you aren't hungry, but you should try to eat something," he said before she could protest. He set the plate and cup on the desk beside her.

Once more, Amy felt her throat constrict. It had been a long time since anyone had looked after her, and Cal's simple gesture made her realize just how alone she'd been for so many years. Amy blinked rapidly to clear the sudden film of moisture from her eyes and then looked up at him. "What about you? I hope you had more than that cookie."

He shrugged. "I nuked something while you changed. Go ahead, eat a few bites at least."

Amy nibbled on the toast and watched as Cal leaned against the back of the couch, hands thrust into his pockets, legs crossed at the ankles. He looked tired, she thought, her gaze softening in sympathy.

"I'm really sorry about dragging you into this, Cal.

After all the stress and strain of the trial, this is the last thing you needed.''

"You didn't drag me into this, Amy. I willingly got involved.''

"Why?''

The question was out before she could stop it, and she felt hot color rise to her cheeks. "Listen. Forget I asked that, okay?''

There was silence for a moment, and when he spoke his voice was cautious. "Why don't you want me to answer that question?''

Because I'm afraid, she cried silently. Afraid of disrupting my carefully planned life. And even more afraid that your answer won't be the one my heart wants to hear.

"I don't think I'm up to dealing with heavy questions tonight,'' she replied instead, her voice quavering slightly.

"I think you're right.'' He stood up and walked slowly toward her, and she stared at him silently, her heart hammering in her chest. For a moment his intense gaze locked with hers, and then he glanced at her plate, now empty except for a few crumbs. "I guess you were hungrier than you thought,'' he said softly.

The husky cadence in his voice made the last swallow of toast stick in her throat. Did the man have even a remote clue how appealing he was? she wondered, trying to ignore her staccato pulse. "I—I guess so,'' she said inanely as she stared back up at him, mesmerized by the banked fire she saw in the depths of his eyes.

He took a deep breath, then cleared his throat. "Come on. You need to get to bed."

Amy didn't object when he took her arm as she stood. She suddenly felt off balance again.

"Do you need to change?" he asked.

She shook her head. "I'm too tired. This will do."

When she reached the bed, she sat down wearily. The physical and emotional upheavals of the past few hours had completely sapped her energy.

Cal waited for her to lie down, but when she continued to simply sit there, shoulders drooping, head bent, he lifted her legs onto the bed, then gently helped position her on her side. He reached for the blanket, pausing in surprise at the hand-stitched quilt that lay at the foot of her bed. The homespun touch seemed out of place in Amy's sophisticated lifestyle.

"Is something wrong?" Amy asked sleepily when he didn't move.

Cal quickly finished drawing up the quilt and tucked it around her shoulders. "I was just admiring your quilt. It reminds me of ones Gram has done. Did you mother make it?"

"No. I did."

He stared down at her in surprise. "You quilt?"

"I grew up on a farm, remember?" Her words were slightly slurred now.

"But I thought you left all that behind."

"Me, too." She sighed. When she spoke again, he had to lean close to hear her fading voice. "Life's funny, isn't it?"

Cal stared down at her. Yeah, life was funny, all right. And surprising. Not to mention confusing.

He reached down and gently brushed a stray strand of hair off her face, his fingers lingering on her soft skin a moment longer than necessary. Then he drew a ragged breath. He had no idea where this thing between them was leading. But he did know one thing. It was time to find out.

Chapter Nine

The delicious smell of fresh-baked cinnamon rolls slowly coaxed Amy out of her deep slumber, and she sighed contentedly, savoring the aroma. What a nice dream. Cinnamon rolls were one of her all-time favorite treats, and it had been a long time since she'd indulged in them. They were *way* too fattening. But at least she could enjoy them in her dreams, where they came calorie free and...

A sudden clatter brought her fully awake, and Amy sat bolt upright, a move she immediately regretted. A wave of dizziness and pain swept over her, and she dropped her head into her hands as yesterday's nightmare events came vividly back to her. And now it seemed she was plunged into yet another nightmare. Someone was in her kitchen! A shiver of alarm raced along her spine, and she groped in the drawer of her nightstand for the pepper spray she'd kept there ever since Cal's mugging. When the world at last stopped spinning, she rose slowly and silently crept to the kitchen, her heart hammering in her chest, pepper spray poised.

If she was inclined to jaw dropping, the sight that greeted her when she peeked around the doorway would have done the trick. Cal was at the stove, concentrating on making what looked like an omelet. His jacket hung over one of the kitchen chairs, and he'd rolled the sleeves of his white shirt up to the elbows. Her gaze lingered on his broad shoulders for a moment before she transferred it to the table, where a plate of cinnamon rolls dripping with icing sent her salivary glands into overdrive.

As Cal reached for a plate, he caught sight of her and, in one swift, discerning glance, assessed her condition. Though her clothes were in disarray, her makeup nonexistent and her hair unkempt, her color was more normal and her eyes looked clearer, he noted with relief. Then his gaze fell on the pepper spray, and he gave her a quizzical grin.

"Your sister told me you had a weakness for cinnamon rolls and anyone who tempted you was in trouble, but don't you think the pepper spray is a little extreme?"

Amy stared at him in confusion. "What are you doing here?"

"Fixing breakfast."

"I can see that. I mean…*why* are you here?"

"I told your sister I'd check on you this morning. And she made me promise to try and get you to eat something." He slid the omelet onto a plate and placed it on the table, then pulled out her chair with a flourish. "Can I tempt you?"

That was definitely a loaded question, Amy thought wryly as she tried to ignore the sudden flutter of her pulse. "Actually, I'm, uh, pretty hungry today," she stammered.

"A good sign," he pronounced, pushing in her chair as she sat down.

"Aren't you eating anything?" she asked as he walked back toward the counter.

"I might try one of those cinnamon rolls with a cup of coffee."

She reached for one herself as he rejoined her, and closed her eyes to savor the first bite. "Mmm! This is heaven!"

Cal chuckled and took a sip of his coffee. "I'll have to tell your sister that her strategy worked."

Amy wrinkled her nose. "She knows me too well. Not that I'm complaining, you understand." She took another big bite and chewed slowly. "Just out of curiosity, may I ask how you got in? Did you call on one of your police connections to jimmy the lock or something?"

"Nothing so dramatic. I left your key on the table by the door when I brought you home last night, so I just borrowed it."

"How late did you stay?"

He shrugged. "A couple of hours after you went to bed. I wanted to make sure you were sleeping okay before I left. By the way, your station called. Somebody named Jarrod. I told him you were asleep, and he said not to worry about coming in for a few days. How's the omelet?''

Amy speared another forkful. "Surprisingly good."

Cal pretended to look offended. "Well, thanks a lot. I do have *some* culinary talent."

She chuckled. "And I suppose you made the cinnamon rolls, too?"

"You've got me there," he admitted with a lopsided grin. "I know a little mom-and-pop bakery that works magic with dough."

"They have my vote," Amy concurred as she helped herself to another roll.

Cal drained his coffee cup and glanced at his watch. "When you finish that, why don't I change your dressing before I head to the office?"

Amy looked at him in surprise. "Cal, you've done more than enough as it is. And you're probably already late for work. I can manage."

"Not easily. You won't even be able to see what you're doing without juggling a mirror in one hand, and I think it's a two-handed job."

She couldn't argue with his logic. "Don't tell me you're a medic, too."

He gave her a disarming grin. "Hardly. Believe it or not, the sight of blood makes me pretty squeamish."

Amy looked at him in surprise. "Honestly?"

"Yep. So much for my macho image."

She smiled, charmed yet again by his lack of pretense. "Then your offer is doubly appreciated. I don't think it's a pretty sight back there. You're not going to pass out on me or anything, are you?''

He chuckled. ''I'll let you know if I feel dizzy.''

He rose and retrieved the gauze and tape, as well as some antiseptic cream, then positioned himself behind her.

''Ready?''

''I guess so.''

Cal carefully eased the tape off her scalp, and though she didn't say a word, he knew by the rigid lines of her body and her white-knuckled grip on her coffee mug that she was hurting. When at last the dressing came free and Cal got his first look at the gouge on the back of her head, he sucked in his breath sharply.

''You okay?'' Amy asked, her own voice strained.

''Yeah.''

''Does it look bad?''

Cal gazed down at the jagged abrasion. It was nearly three inches long, caked with dried blood and framed by angry, inflamed skin. ''Bad'' was an understatement.

''Could be worse,'' he replied, striving to keep his voice light as he reached for the gauze. ''I think I'll clean it up a little before I put the cream on, though.'' He walked over to the sink and dampened the gauze, giving himself a moment to recover from his first look at the cut. He hadn't been kidding when he told Amy he was no medic. He didn't like blood. Never had. Especially when it was on someone he cared about. And seeing her injury in living color only brought home to him again how close she had come to something more serious.

He took his time at the sink, and by the time he repositioned himself behind her, he felt calmer. "This will probably hurt," he said apologetically.

"I'm sure it will. But I can handle it," she said with more bravado than she felt.

Cal was sure she could. Amy Winter was one tough lady. But he didn't want to test her limits, so he cleaned off the dried blood as carefully as he could until at last the long row of stitches was revealed. He paused once when she winced, and let his hand drop to her shoulder.

"I'm okay," she said shakily.

He waited a moment, then carefully applied the cream and rebandaged the wound, using a much smaller piece of gauze than the one applied by the emergency room staff. "I think they overdid it with the bandage at the hospital. In fact, you should be able to disguise that premature bald spot pretty well with your hair," he teased, hoping to distract her.

When she made no comment, he finished up quickly, then came around and squatted beside her. Her face looked strained, and slightly paler than when she had first come into the kitchen, and he reached over and touched her cheek gently, his gaze tender. "I'm sorry if I hurt you," he said softly.

She drew in a deep breath. "It's okay. There's no way around it for the next few days, I guess. I'll just try to get a lot of rest, and hopefully it will heal faster."

He hesitated for a moment, then cleared his throat. "I have a suggestion about the rest part."

He seemed suddenly...*nervous* was the word that came to mind, and she looked at him curiously. "What?"

He didn't answer her question immediately. Instead, he rose and returned to his seat, where he wrapped his hands around his empty coffee cup. Now he really had her attention. "What is it, Cal?"

He looked over at her. The idea had come to him late last night, and at the time it had seemed inspired. Now, in the light of day, he wasn't so sure. But he had already decided that he could no longer ignore the attraction between them, and this was an ideal opportunity to test the waters.

"After the trial ended, my boss suggested I take a few days off and go home to the mountains to recharge my batteries. I'm leaving tomorrow. Your boss told me last night that they want you to take a few days off to rest and recuperate, too. Since there's no better place for that than the Smokies, I was wondering if you—if you might like to join me. The mountains can do wonders for your mental and physical health."

Amy stared at him, clearly stunned by the invitation. Cal had expected her to be surprised, had known it was a gamble. And the odds of her accepting seemed to be dropping rapidly with each second that ticked by. When the silence lengthened, he shifted uncomfortably.

"Listen, I know this is unexpected. Why don't you think about it today and give me your answer tonight?'' he suggested. "I'll stop by on my way home to change the dressing again.''

Amy hardly heard his addendum. She was still too busy trying to process the unexpected invitation. "Did you just ask me to go home with you?'' she said carefully.

"Yeah. There's plenty of room in Gram's cabin. I know it's not the Caribbean or the exotic resorts you like, but it's quiet and restful. And it might do you a lot of good.''

His voice was casual, but Amy could sense his tension as she considered the invitation. While she wanted to explore the possibilities of their relationship, this was a giant step. One she wasn't altogether sure she was ready to take. She'd figured on easing into this thing, not jumping in feetfirst. And a few days in the mountains, with Cal's family and on his turf, was definitely feetfirst. On the other hand, maybe that's exactly what she should do. She'd probably find out pretty quick whether there was any potential between them. As she tried to weigh the pros and cons of accepting, her head began to ache, and she reached up to rub her temples.

"How long will you be gone?'' she asked, stalling.

"Until Wednesday night.''

"Let me check with my station and find out just how much time I can take, okay?''

"Fair enough. I'll be here about six. And don't worry about food. I'll pick up a pizza.''

She looked at him and shook her head. No matter what happened between them, one thing was clear.

"You're an amazing man, Cal Richards," she said softly.

He felt his neck grow red, even as his heart grew warm. "I have to eat, anyway." He rose and reached for his coat. "Take it easy today, okay?"

She nodded. "I don't think I'm up to doing much else."

He laid a hand gently on her shoulder, and for a moment their gazes locked—and sizzled. Amy's mouth went dry; she moistened her lips with her tongue. Cal's gaze dropped, and she heard his sharply indrawn breath, saw his Adam's apple bob convulsively. Then, without another word, he turned and left.

"Amy! I've been praying for you ever since I woke up! If you hadn't called me in the next ten minutes, I was going to call *you!*"

Amy pulled her knees up and snuggled into the corner of the couch. "I didn't want to wake you. I know you've been sleeping later since you got pregnant."

"Not this morning. I hardly closed my eyes all night, thinking about you. Did you call Mom?"

"Yes. She hadn't heard anything about it, so I downplayed the whole incident as much as possible. I don't think she was too worried."

"Unlike your sister, who saw it all in living color."

"I'm sorry, Kate. I still can't believe it made national news."

"I can. It was a pretty heroic thing to do."

"Anyone would have done the same."

"But they didn't. You were the only one."

"You sound like Cal. And thanks a lot for telling him about the cinnamon rolls. I probably put on five pounds in the last two hours."

"He brought them!" Her sister sounded delighted.

"Yeah. Bright and early. Almost too early, in fact. I heard noises in the kitchen and thought it was an intruder. I almost zapped him with the pepper spray."

"Amy! You didn't!"

"I said 'almost.' Good thing I didn't. It would have ruined the cinnamon rolls. Not to mention the omelet."

"He made you an omelet?" her sister said reverently.

"Yes. And a very good one, I might add."

"This man sounds like a keeper, Amy."

Amy sighed. "Yeah, he does, doesn't he? The thing is, I'm not sure I have time for romance, Kate. And besides, we're so different. He's a country boy at heart, and I like the bright lights. I don't see how it could ever work."

"You'll never know if you don't give it a chance. What do you have to lose?"

My heart, Amy replied silently. But her spoken words were different. "You're assuming that he's interested."

"A man doesn't show up at a hospital emergency room if he's not interested, Amy. I bet if you gave him any encouragement, he'd pursue this."

Amy sighed. "It seems you're right again, dear sister. He does want to pursue it. The station gave me a few days off, and he invited me to go to the mountains with him.''

There was a long beat of silence, and when Kate spoke, her tone was suddenly cautious. ''Look, Amy, maybe this isn't such a good idea after all. Up till now, everything you've told me about this guy has led me to believe that he's got his head on straight and has pretty solid moral values. But if he's inviting you to shack up with him for the weekend, then—''

''Hold on, Kate,'' Amy interrupted with a laugh. ''Trust me, that isn't his style. We'd be staying with his grandmother.''

The relief in Kate's voice was obvious. ''Well, thank goodness! You're going, aren't you?''

''I don't know.''

Again there was a moment of silence. ''It wouldn't be because you're afraid, would it?'' Kate finally asked, her voice gentle.

Amy frowned. ''What do you mean?''

''I don't know if I can explain exactly,'' Kate said hesitantly. ''It's just that…well, all these years I've watched you single-mindedly go after what you want. I've admired you in many ways, even envied your drive and commitment at times, as well as your ability to stay focused. You just didn't let anything into your life that could deter you from capturing the golden ring. But I honestly can't say that you've ever seemed really happy or…or content. And I think maybe you've missed some good things along the way, all in the name of your career. I'm not saying career isn't important, Amy. You've worked hard and done well, and I know that means a lot to you. But it's not everything. And maybe it's not even the most important thing.'' She paused and took a deep breath. ''I guess what it comes down to is this. I don't want you to pass up a chance at love just because the guy came along at the wrong time or is a little different than what you expected.''

Kate's comments mirrored her own recent thoughts so closely that for a moment Amy was too surprised to speak.

''Amy?'' Kate's concerned voice came over the wire. ''Listen, I didn't mean to offend you, but...''

''It's okay,'' Amy assured her sister. ''You just hit a little too close to home. I guess maybe I am afraid. After investing so much of my life and myself in my career—pretty much to the exclusion of all else—it's pretty scary to think about changing course. Especially when I've been so sure about my destination.''

''I know it's hard for you. You've always been the type to hang on tenaciously once you set your mind to something. Remember the violin?''

Amy chuckled. ''Yeah.''

''You drove us nuts at home. Even though the teacher kept telling you that it just wasn't your instrument, you were determined to be the next Itzhak Perlman. We all deserve a special place in heaven for putting up with that screeching for...how long? Four years? Five?''

''It was only two.''

''Well, it seemed at least twice that long.''

Amy laughed. ''I must admit, you guys were pretty good sports. And you're right. I have a hard time letting go, once I make my mind up to go after something.''

''Well, let me tell you, we all got down on our knees and thanked the Lord when you took up quilting. It was the answer to our prayers. And you would never have discovered you had a talent for it if you hadn't gone to that meeting for Mom. In fact, until then, whenever she brought it up you just laughed it off. You said it wouldn't be a good fit. But you found out differently once you tried it. I guess all I'm saying about Cal is that maybe it's the same kind of thing. It might not look like a good fit on the surface, but you might be surprised if you give it a chance.''

''You know something, Kate?''

''What?''

''You're one sharp lady.''

Kate chuckled. ''I wish you'd thought that when we were teenagers. It would have prevented quite a few squabbles. So you don't mind the advice, then?''

''No.''

''Then can I give you one more piece?''

''Sure.''

''I know you haven't kept up with your faith these past few years. But it wouldn't hurt to ask for a little guidance. The Lord always comes through, you know.''

''Frankly, Kate, I don't think He even remembers my name.''

''Of course He does. That's the nice thing about the Lord, Amy. Even if we ignore Him, He never ignores us. But enough preaching. You'll let me know what you decide about the trip, won't you?''

"Absolutely. Just as soon as I know myself."

Amy sat there for a long time after she rang off, weighing the pros and cons of accepting Cal's invitation. When the minutes ticked by and she didn't seem to be any closer to a resolution, she decided to take Kate's advice and try asking for guidance from a higher power.

It had been a long time since she'd prayed, and at first she felt awkward. But as she closed her eyes and struggled to express her chaotic thoughts in the silence of her heart, the words suddenly came.

Dear Lord, I know You haven't heard from me in a while. It's not that I stopped believing. I've just been too busy to take time for prayer. Or, I guess more truthfully, I just haven't made time for prayer, the way Cal has. Anyway, he's the reason I'm coming to You now. I like him, Lord. A lot. But I'm afraid if I let him get too close, it could change my life forever. On the other hand, Kate could be right. I might be letting something really good slip away if I don't pursue this. I'm confused, Lord. I need Your help. I know I've been a wayward soul for too long, but I'm going to try to find my way back to You. And in the meantime, please guide me to make the right decision about this.

When Amy opened her eyes, she had no magic solution to her dilemma. But somehow her burden seemed lighter. And she had a feeling that by the time Cal arrived that evening, she'd be ready to give him an answer.

As the first blue-hued mountains appeared on the distant horizon, Cal drew in a slow, deep, cleansing

breath. The familiar and comforting sense of home-
coming swept over him, and he turned to glance at
Amy, anxious to share this moment with her. But she
was still sleeping soundly.

His gaze softened as it lingered on her face, and
only with great effort did he turn his attention back
to the road. He was glad she was sleeping. She'd
looked exhausted when he'd arrived to pick her up
this morning. Though her wound seemed to be heal-
ing nicely, the skin around the abrasion was badly
bruised from the trauma. Apparently she'd inadvertently turned on her back a few times during the night,
and the pressure on her tender skin had rudely—and
painfully—jolted her awake. Though she'd tried to
keep up a breezy conversation during the first hour
or so of the trip, the gentle lulling motion of the car
had eventually made her drowsy, and she'd drifted
off. That had been almost three hours ago.

Cal didn't mind. He was just glad she'd accepted
his invitation. It had seemed touch-and-go for a while,
and he'd been prepared to press her if she'd turned
him down when he'd arrived with the pizza. But surprisingly she had said yes with no further discussion.
She'd mentioned that she'd talked with her sister that
day, and if Kate was responsible for Amy's decision,
then he owed her. Big time. Because the more he'd
thought about it, the more confident he was that his
middle-of-the-night inspiration to invite her home was
sound. Though they'd never discussed—or even acknowledged—the attraction between them, it was as
real as the mountains looming ahead. And it was time

to face it. Here, away from the distractions of their everyday lives, perhaps they could both come to grips with their feelings.

Amy made a soft sound, and he glanced toward her just as her eyelids flickered open.

"Hi, sleepyhead," he teased with a smile.

She blinked and rubbed her eyes in an endearing little-girl gesture that tugged at his heart.

"Hi." She peered at her watch, and then quickly straightened up, her eyes widening. "Have I been asleep for three hours?"

"Uh-huh."

"Oh, Cal, I'm sorry! I meant to keep you company during the drive."

"You needed the rest. And I've made this drive alone more times than I can count. It's only five or six hours. It gives me a chance to unwind and let the cares of the city slip away."

Amy gazed out the window and scanned the landscape appreciatively. "It's beautiful here."

"We're just in the foothills. It's even better closer to the park. We should be at Gram's cabin in less than an hour."

They chatted companionably during the remainder of the trip, and in what seemed only a few minutes, Cal turned into a gravel driveway that led toward a cabin.

"This is home," he said quietly, stopping the car for a moment to gaze at the scene.

The cabin was fairly rustic, separated from the road by a large meadow. Colorful flowers spilled from planters along the porch railing, and a grove of pine trees seemed to come right up to the back door. In an adjacent pasture a horse grazed contentedly against a serene backdrop of misty blue-hued mountains.

The peace of the scene stole over Amy, and for the first time in a long while she felt the always-present tension in her shoulders begin to ease. There was a calmness to this place that made the location seem far away from the hustle and bustle of her world—not only in miles, but in spirit. The quiet—broken only by an occasional birdcall—and the beauty of nature were like a balm for the soul, and Amy drew in a long, slow breath.

When she turned to Cal, he was watching her with an enigmatic expression on his face. She sensed that he was waiting for her to comment, and she struggled to find the words to capture her first reaction.

"I think I already understand why you love this place so much," she said softly. "It's like a world apart. There's so much beauty and calmness here, and a kind of...I don't know how to describe it exactly. It's like a special tranquillity that you just breathe in."

His smile warmed her to her toes. "I hoped you might see it that way." Their gazes held for a long moment, and then he turned and nodded toward the porch. "I think the welcoming committee is waiting."

Amy followed his gaze. Two people stood by the railing, waving.

"Gram and my dad," Cal explained as he put the car in gear.

As they closed the distance to the cabin, Amy studied the two people who were so special to Cal. Interestingly enough, neither was exactly what she'd expected. Though there was a resemblance between Cal and his father, the older man was much shorter than his son, and slightly stooped. His thinning hair was mostly gray, but there were enough sandy-colored strands left to provide a clue to its original color. He had a nice but careworn face and kind eyes. *Quiet* and *gentle* were the words that came to mind as Amy looked at him.

Cal's grandmother was also thin, but she radiated energy. She was dressed in jeans, her white hair closely cropped, and anticipation flashed in her eyes. Amy could almost imagine her hopping from one foot to the other in her excitement, an image so "ungrandmotherly," it brought a smile to her lips. By the time Cal stopped the car and started to alight, the older woman was waiting at his door.

"My, it's good to see you, son!" she said, hugging him fiercely. "You've been way too scarce."

Cal's father followed more slowly, a pipe in one hand, and patiently waited his turn to greet his son. When Cal at last stepped free of Gram's enthusiastic embrace, he reached out and pulled his father into a bear hug.

"Hello, Dad."

"Hello, son. It's good to have you home."

The two men stood like that for a long minute, and Amy could sense the bond of love between them. In fact, the three of them shared a circle of love that suddenly made her feel like an intruder. She didn't belong here. Cal should have used this rare break to spend time with his family, not entertain her. Maybe he was already regretting the invitation. Maybe she should...

As if sensing their visitor's sudden discomfort, Gram leaned in the open door of the driver's side and smiled warmly.

"You must be Amy." She held out her hand, and Amy's was engulfed in a firm clasp. "I'm Gram. Or Amanda. Whatever you prefer. I hope you'll excuse us. We're kind of a gushy bunch when we haven't seen each other for weeks. Usually we have a little more decorum when it comes to public displays of affection." She turned back to the two men and clapped Cal on the back. "Break it up, you two. Let's go inside so our guest can settle in and I can get dinner on the table."

Cal smiled and leaned in to look at Amy. "Sit tight. I'll get your door."

Before she could protest, he strode around to her side and pulled it open, Gram and his father close on his heels.

"Gram, Dad, this is Amy Winter. Amy, I'd like you to meet my family."

Cal's father stepped forward shyly and took her hand. "I'm very pleased to meet you, Amy. Cal has told us a lot of nice things about you."

She smiled at the older man's courtly manner. "I've heard good things about you, too. I'm glad we had this chance to meet."

Gram stepped forward next and enveloped her in a hug. She was small and wiry, but there was strength in her arms—and in her face. "We're mighty glad you came to visit, Amy. And honored. Cal told us all about how you got hurt saving that little boy. You feeling okay after that long ride?''

Before she could reply, Cal spoke up. ''She's tired. And I'm sure she's hungry. We didn't stop to eat on the way up.''

''Well, say no more. Dinner's on the stove. Some good food and rest will fix you up in no time, Amy. And the mountain air will do wonders for you. Clear your lungs of all that smog you breathe down in Atlanta.''

Cal smiled. ''It's good to be back, Gram.''

She returned the smile, and when she spoke, her voice was warm and rang with a quiet sincerity. ''Well, we're mighty glad to *have* you back. Welcome home—both of you.''

Cal glanced at Amy. For a moment their gazes met and held. And as he wondered if Gram's words were somehow prophetic, Amy had the oddest feeling. She'd never been anywhere near the Smokies before. But for some inexplicable reason, it really did feel like coming home.

Chapter Ten

Two hours later, stuffed with fried chicken, mashed potatoes, homemade biscuits with honey and warm-from-the-oven apple pie with ice cream, Amy thought she was going to explode.

"I haven't eaten that much since…well, maybe never," she groaned as she and Cal rocked gently on the porch swing.

He smiled. "Gram's a great cook."

"Agreed. I feel guilty about not helping with the cleanup, though."

"Don't. Hospitality is Gram's middle name. We'll have more luck pitching in after we've been around for a few days."

The slowly-sinking sun cast a golden glow on the landscape, and Amy sighed contentedly as the swing moved rhythmically back and forth. "It's nice here," she murmured.

"I thought you'd be missing the city lights by now," Cal teased.

"I'm used to rural life, remember?"

"But you don't like it."

"I wouldn't want to go back to the farm," she conceded. "But this is different."

When he didn't respond, she turned to find him studying her, a cryptic expression on his face.

"What are you thinking?" she asked curiously.

He seemed momentarily taken aback by the question, but he recovered quickly. "Just wondering how you're feeling. How's the head?"

She glanced away. "Okay."

"Amy…"

She looked back at him, caught off guard by his gently chiding tone. "What?"

"The truth."

She tilted her head and studied his deep brown eyes, a frown creasing her brow. "How do you know I'm not telling the truth?"

He shrugged. "Your tone. Your body language. I don't know how I know. I just know."

She shook her head. "No wonder you're such a good attorney. You have amazing powers of perception."

"Only with certain people." Before she could ponder that remark, he distracted her by draping his arm around her shoulders and pulling her close. "Lean your head against me and relax."

Relax? With her cheek pressed against the soft cotton of his shirt, the steady beat of his heart beneath her ear? With the faint scent of his aftershave filling her nostrils? With the angle of his jaw brushing against her forehead, the faint end-of-day stubble creating a sensuous texture against her skin? He must be kidding!

But as they swung gently back and forth, and dusk slowly deepened, she did relax. Cal could feel the gradual easing of her tense muscles, knew exactly when she finally dropped her defenses and simply gave herself up to the moment. He also knew she was afraid, just as he was, and he understood her caution. But he also knew—in fact, was even beginning to hope—that perhaps their fears were groundless. And before they left the mountains, he intended to find out.

"Amanda, these are gorgeous!" Amy held up yet another intricate hand-stitched quilt, her eyes alight.

Gram looked pleased. "The ladies do a wonderful job," she agreed. "But all of our craftspeople are talented."

Amy carefully laid the quilt down and glanced around the attractive and bustling craft co-op. Cal had told her how Gram had started it years ago to give locals an outlet for their work—as well as a chance to supplement often meager incomes—and how she had worked tirelessly to build it into a thriving business that visitors now sought out. Amy could see why. The quality of the merchandise was excellent, as was the variety.

"I'm impressed, Amanda," she said honestly. "Cal told me about this, but I had no idea it was anything on this scale."

Gram waved the praise aside. "I like to keep busy. And if I can help my neighbors at the same time, all the better. I'm glad it worked out for everybody."

"Ready to go?" Cal came up beside Amy and draped an arm across her shoulders, something he'd been doing quite a lot of since they arrived.

She turned to look up at him, melting in the warmth of his eyes. Her voice suddenly deserted her, and she simply nodded.

"We'll be home in a couple of hours, Gram," Cal said.

"Don't hurry. I'll be here awhile yet, and your dad's at a church committee meeting. You give Amy a good tour, show her some of our great scenery. But don't wear her out," she warned.

Cal smiled. "Don't worry. I'll take good care of her." He let his arm drop from her shoulders, but in the next instant captured her hand in a warm clasp as they headed for his car.

It was just another manifestation of the change that Amy had sensed in him almost from the moment he'd picked her up at her apartment. Until then, he'd held his feelings carefully in check. She figured that, like her, he'd probably overanalyzed the situation and arrived at the logical conclusion that nothing could develop between them. But neither had reckoned with the power of the heart or the strength of their mutual attraction, she admitted. She was still waging the fight between logic and emotion, but it appeared that Cal, at least for the duration of this trip, was letting his heart dictate his actions. Which suggested some interesting possibilities, Amy realized, as a delicious shiver of excitement swept over her.

Once they were on the road, Cal took on the role of tour guide as they drove along some of the many scenic roads in the park. Finally he pulled into a parking area and turned to her.

"Do you feel like a little walk?"

"Sure. I even dressed for outdoor activity."

"I noticed." Her cotton blouse softly hugged her curves, nipped in at her slender waist by a hemp belt that emphasized her trim figure. Her long legs were encased in formfitting jeans that highlighted her lean, athletic build. But despite the ruggedness of her attire, she looked incredibly feminine—and very, very appealing. Yes, he'd definitely noticed, he thought wryly.

"I'm not exactly up to mountain climbing, though," she cautioned, redirecting his train of thought.

"What I had in mind was a nice, easy walk along that stream." He nodded to a tumbling brook, just visible through the trees.

"Sounds just my speed."

As they set off, he once more took her hand, and Amy felt a lightness of heart that was at once strange and wonderful. Here, in this place, so far removed from the normal routine of her life, she suddenly felt free to let her feelings bubble to the surface—and to savor them instead of fear them. She liked being with Cal, liked the feel of his strong, sure fingers entwined with hers, liked the sense of being cared for that his presence invoked. They were good feelings, new feelings, feelings that at once both frightened and stirred her. And though she still didn't know where this was leading, she did know one thing with absolute certainty: her decision to accept his invitation had been the right one.

They walked quietly for some time, the silence broken only by the splashing water and the call of birds. When at last the stream widened into a small pool fed by a tiered waterfall, Cal paused and looked down at her.

"This is one of my favorite spots. The waterfall isn't as dramatic as others in the park, so it gets fewer visitors. Usually I have the place to myself. Would you like to sit for a while?"

"Yes. It's lovely here."

Cal led her to a large, flat rock dappled by the sun. She sat and drew her knees up, wrapped her arms around them and sighed contentedly.

He chuckled as he joined her. "My sentiments exactly."

She turned to look at him. He, too, was dressed in jeans that hugged his slim hips and outlined his muscular legs. The sleeves of his cotton shirt were rolled to the elbows, revealing an expanse of sun-browned forearm flecked with dark hair. As he leaned back, putting his palms on the rock behind him, his shirt stretched tautly across his broad chest. Amy swallowed and, with an effort, transferred her gaze to his face. He had closed his eyes and tilted his head back to the sun, and she was struck again by the change in him since they'd arrived in the mountains. All evidence of strain had vanished, and he seemed completely happy and at ease—like this was where he belonged, she realized, inexplicably troubled by the thought.

He turned at that moment, and his eyebrows rose quizzically. "Why the frown?"

She dismissed his question with a shrug, unsure of the answer herself. "This place is good for you, you know."

"Why do you say that?"

"You seem more…content here, I guess. And laid-back. In the city you always seem a little tense and on edge, like you never really relax."

"I have a demanding job."

"Yeah, I know all about demanding jobs," she replied wryly.

"Yours seems particularly demanding. Not to mention dangerous."

She shrugged. "Demanding, always. Dangerous, rarely."

"Forgive me if I can't quite accept that. Not after this." He leaned over and gently touched her head.

"That's the exception, Cal. I'm not in this work to get killed. Trust me."

"But you don't hold back, either. Do you ever do anything halfway?"

She tipped her head and considered the question. "I've never thought of it quite that way before, but no, I guess not. I'm the type who does everything full-out—you know, the old 'Anything worth doing is worth doing well' philosophy. And I can't just stand by when people are in trouble, either. That's always been one of my weaknesses."

"I'd hardly call it that."

"It is in my business. We're supposed to report stories—not become part of them."

"Then maybe you're in the wrong business."

His quiet remark hit too close to home, but she forced herself to smile. "Well, if I switched careers you'd have one less reporter to hate," she countered, striving for a light tone.

He looked at her, and the intensity of his gaze made her breath catch in her throat. "I was wrong to make such a sweeping generalization, Amy. And I was especially wrong about one particular reporter. In fact, *hate* is the last word that comes to mind when I think of you."

The husky cadence and intimate tone of his voice, along with the sudden warmth in his eyes, scared her, and she glanced away nervously.

"I liked your grandmother's shop," she said with forced brightness. "Some of the things are so…"

The touch of his hand on her arm made the words stick in her throat.

"Amy."

His voice was gentle but firm, and she drew a shaky breath. They'd been dodging this thing between them for too long, and Cal was finally facing it. But it took her several more moments to gather the courage to look at him. When she did, the tenderness in his eyes made her heart catch, then race on.

"Don't be afraid," he said quietly.

Her throat constricted, and she swallowed with difficulty. "You sound like Kate."

"How so?"

Amy broke eye contact and dropped her cheek to her knees. "She told me I was afraid, too. And you— you're both right."

Cal slid closer and took her cold hand, cradling it in the warmth of his clasp. "You know what? So am I. But there's something between us too powerful to ignore. I've seen it in your face. And I've spent too many sleepless nights grappling with it. We need to deal with this thing."

She looked at him again. "We're too different, Cal."

"I used to think so. I'm not as sure anymore."

"But we want different things out of life."

"Do we?"

She drew a ragged breath. "Even if we had the same priorities, this isn't a good time for me. I'm still trying to build my career."

"It's not the best time for me, either. I'm struggling with some pretty heavy decisions and, frankly, I don't need the distraction. But I've got it whether I want it or not. Because you, lovely lady, are one big distraction."

He reached over then and touched her face, his gaze locked on hers. The feel of his fingertips against her skin sent her pulse off the scale, and she closed her eyes as he slowly traced the line of her jaw and the curve of her cheek. When he let his fingertips glide over her lips with a feather-light touch, she moaned softly.

"Oh, Amy, I've wanted to do this for so long," he said hoarsely. And then he pulled her gently into his arms, one hand in the small of her back, the other beneath her hair, cradling her neck. For several long moments, he just held her tenderly, taking time to simply relish the long-dreamed-of closeness. He could feel her trembling, but she didn't pull away, and he stroked her back reassuringly.

"It's okay, sweetheart," he murmured, his lips against her hair. "I'm just as scared as you are. We'll take this slow and easy, okay?"

Amy wasn't at all sure it was okay. This whole thing was moving far faster than she'd anticipated. But she could no longer deny her feelings for this man. She cared about him—deeply. Okay, so maybe this wasn't the best time in her life for romance. Maybe Cal didn't exactly fit the profile she'd created of her "ideal man." She'd always imagined that someday she'd be half of a "power" couple, living a glittering, jet-set type life. Yet Cal had no interest in that. He liked things simple and unpretentious, and his priorities clearly didn't include power or prestige or worldly success. Amy's did. Or had. Oddly enough, she wasn't so sure they did anymore.

But she put those thoughts aside for the moment. As she savored the feel of Cal's strong arms about her, she felt safe, protected, cherished—and free. Which was odd. Even in a perfect relationship, she'd always imagined that one was less free because the partner's needs always had to be considered and accommodated. But for the first time, she considered the possibility that maybe she'd had it all wrong. Because here, wrapped in his arms, she sensed a love so supportive, so unconditional, that it was liberating, freeing her to take risks she might otherwise not consider because she always knew she had the safety net of his arms—and his love—to catch her if she fell. It was an astounding revelation, one to be carefully thought through later, when her mind was behaving rationally. Certainly not now, when the feel of his hard chest against her soft curves was driving all lucid thoughts from her brain.

Cal felt the tension in her body slowly ease, and he pulled back slightly to gaze down at her, framing her face with his long, lean fingers as he brushed his thumbs over her cheeks. She looked up at him, her deep green eyes slightly dazed—but also trusting. It was a look that said, "I don't know where this is leading. I'm not even sure if it's a good idea. But I care for you. I trust you. And, at least for the moment, my heart is yours."

Cal's throat tightened. He'd dated any number of women through the years, but none had looked at him in quite this same way. And given how hard Amy was fighting this thing, he was even more deeply touched. He drew a long, unsteady breath, then combed his fingers through her hair, careful to avoid the back of her head. When he lifted her soft tresses aside to brush his lips against her nape, he heard her sigh softly. And as he slowly kissed her forehead, then each eyelid, making a slow, tantalizing journey toward his ultimate destination, he felt her hands clutch his back convulsively.

When at last he claimed her lips, her surprisingly ardent response almost snapped the tenuous hold he had on his emotions. She gave as she lived—fully, completely, no holding back, without pretense or reservation. His initial touch, gentle and exploratory, rapidly grew fierce and demanding as he gave way to the hunger that had consumed him for weeks.

Amy had been kissed before, but never with such a mix of tenderness and passion. It took her breath away and sent her world spinning out of orbit as a long, sweet shiver of delight swept over her. When Cal's hands moved over her back, molding her slender frame against the muscular contours of his body, she made no protest. The tension between them had been building for weeks, and it was pure joy to at last release her feelings. Strangely enough, Amy felt that she'd been waiting for this moment not just for the last few weeks, but all her life. Here, in this man's arms, she felt somehow as if she'd come home.

When at last Cal pulled reluctantly away, Amy shakily raised her fingers to her lips, which still throbbed from his touch. She stared at him dazedly, stunned by the storm of emotion that had swept over her.

Cal tried to draw a deep breath, only to discover that his lungs weren't working very well. Nor was his heart, which was thudding as hard as if he'd just run a thousand-yard dash. He ran unsteady fingers through his hair, then reached over and took her hand.

"Are you okay?" His voice was as uneven as his pulse.

"Just make the world stop spinning, okay?" she whispered.

Somehow he summoned up a crooked grin. "Sure. Just as soon as I come back to Earth."

Now it was Amy's turn to try for a smile. "Well, I guess we know now that on at least one level we're compatible."

"That's putting it mildly."

"Cal, I—I've never experienced anything quite like that before. It was like—like an earthquake and fireworks and Christmas morning all in one."

He smiled, and the warmth in his eyes made her tingle all over. "I couldn't have said it better myself."

"But…" Her look of wonder changed to a frown and she distractedly brushed her hair back from her face. "I mean, where do we go from here? I'm not sure I can handle this kind of…intensity…knowing that we may not have any kind of future together."

He studied her for a moment, a slight frown now marring his own brow. "You sound like you've already decided we don't."

"I didn't mean it that way. It's just that I've always been practical, and I see a lot of obstacles in our path."

"Obstacles can be overcome if two people are committed to finding a way around them."

"I'd like to believe that."

"Then do. Let me tell you something, Amy." He laced his fingers with hers and cupped the back of her neck with his other hand, massaging gently, his eyes only inches from hers. "I don't know why our paths crossed at this particular time in our lives. I don't know why we feel the way we do about each other, given our apparent differences. But I do know this. It happened for a reason. And I'm willing to put this in the Lord's hands and trust that He'll reveal that reason to us in His own time and in His own way. Until then, I'm inclined to let this develop. And to be perfectly honest, I'm not sure I could walk away now even if I wanted to.''

Amy gazed into his sincere, caring eyes, and knew she was lost. She couldn't walk away, either. And maybe he was right. Maybe the best way to deal with this was to simply trust in the Lord to give them guidance. She hadn't done that for a long time. But she was in over her head on this one, and she needed help from a higher power to resolve her dilemma. At last she drew a deep breath and nodded.

"Okay. I'm willing to give it a try."

His relieved smile chased the tension from his face. "Good. I was prepared to argue my case with some pretty convincing evidence, but I'm glad we were able to settle out of court."

She smiled, a teasing light suddenly flitting through her eyes. "Do you think maybe you might want to present some of that evidence, anyway, Counselor?"

For a moment he looked surprised, then a deep chuckle rumbled out of his chest. "I think that could be arranged."

And as his lips once more closed over hers, Amy prayed that they would somehow find a way to resolve their differences. Because one thing was becoming very clear to her. She was rapidly falling in love with Cal Richards. And it was getting harder and harder to imagine the rest of her life without him.

Cal glanced at Amy sitting beside him in the pew, still amazed that she'd agreed to go to Sunday services with his family. He'd told her last night that she didn't have to do it for him, that if they were going to make this thing between them work, neither should feel compelled to do something out of character just to please the other person. But she'd assured him that she was doing it for herself, that it was something she'd decided even before they'd acknowledged their feelings for each other.

Gazing at her now as she raptly listened to Reverend Mitchell's sermon, Cal couldn't doubt her sincerity. She seemed genuinely interested in what the kindly minister was saying—as *he* should be, he reminded himself sternly, refocusing his attention on the pastor.

"And so it is that the Lord gives us choices. Free will is truly a wonderful gift—but it can also be a hardship. Because sometimes we must make difficult decisions. Decisions those we love do not agree with. Decisions that will change our lives forever, in ways we cannot fathom at the time. Decisions that we know in our hearts we *must* make in order to be true to ourselves and to the Lord.

"But we never have to make those decisions alone, my friends. For as Matthew tells us, the Lord stands ready to help us if we simply make the request. 'Ask, and it shall be given to you; seek, and you shall find; knock, and it shall be opened to you.'

"As all of us know, today's world is not always compatible with the ways of the Lord. It's easy to lose sight of priorities in this material age. Temptations face us at every turn. But on your journey through this world, I encourage you to cling to the things that truly last—faith, hope and love. For these will sustain you into eternal life, long after the fleeting glories and gratifications of this world have faded away.

"So as you face the choices in your life, ask yourself if your decision is consistent with those three things—for yourself and for others. And when you answer that question honestly, your decision will be clear—though not always easy. But remember, my friends—the Lord never promised us an easy life in this world if we followed his teachings—only eternal life in the next. And His grace to help us along the way in this one.

"And now let us pray...."

As the minister led the congregation in prayer, Amy was struck by the odd coincidence that Reverend Mitchell would have chosen this weekend to speak on the subject of choices and priorities. Or *was* it a coincidence? she wondered, lost in thought.

Only when a beautiful, soaring solo voice began to sing did she return to her surroundings. She glanced over at the choir, her eyes widening when she realized that the voice belonged to Amanda. When she turned to Cal, she found him watching her with a smile.

"Why didn't you tell me your grandmother could sing like that?" she whispered in awe.

"I thought it would be more fun to surprise you," he murmured.

"*Surprise* is hardly the word. She could be a professional."

"Ask her about it sometime," Cal said quietly as the congregation joined in on the refrain.

Amy intended to do just that, but after the service

they were kept busy as Cal greeted and introduced her to a number of old friends.

"Cal! I thought that was you!"

They turned to find a fortyish, slightly balding man approaching them. Cal grinned and held out his hand. "Tony Jackson! I don't believe it! What are you doing here?"

"I'm home for the weekend visiting my folks. Cindy took the kids to her parents' for a few days, but I couldn't get away from the station for more than a couple of days."

"Station?"

"Didn't you know? I operate a Christian cable station out of Knoxville now."

"No kidding! Last I heard you were a business tycoon jetting all over the world."

The man grinned. "Being an investment banker hardly qualifies me as a business tycoon. It had its exciting moments, though. But I found better work— not more profitable, you understand, but more worthwhile." He nodded to Amy. "Are you going to introduce your friend, or do I have to take the initiative?"

Cal put his arm around Amy and drew her forward with an apologetic grin. "Sorry about that. I was just so surprised to see you. Amy, this is Tony Jackson. We grew up together. Tony, Amy Winter. You two have something in common, it seems. Amy is a broadcast journalist in Atlanta." When he named the station, Tony's eyebrows rose.

"I'm impressed," he said.

Amy smiled and shook her head dismissively.

"Don't be. I'm still working my way up the proverbial ladder."

"You have to be pretty exceptional to even *get* on that ladder, from what I hear."

"'Exceptional' is a good word for Amy," Cal said, his warm gaze connecting with hers briefly. She felt a flush spread over her face as she turned back to Tony.

"He's being kind," she demurred.

"Honest is more likely. Cal always had great judgment. Listen, I don't suppose you'd consider it, but if you ever have any interest in exploring a different kind of reporting, I'd love to talk to you. Of course, we can't compete with the glamour or salaries the big guys offer. We're in the early stages, and building a station from the ground up is a gradual process. Still, slowly but surely we're finding talented people who believe in our message enough to make a commitment to our work and sacrifice some of the worldly gain."

Amy smiled. "I'm flattered. But I'm pretty happy right now where I am."

Tony grinned engagingly. "Well, it was worth a try." He held out his hand, and shook hers, then Cal's. "Good to see you, pal. Keep in touch."

"I will. And good luck with your new venture."

Tony's grin widened. "We can't miss, you know. Remember—if God is with you, who can be against you?" With a wave he sauntered off.

Cal turned to Amy, but was interrupted by Reverend Mitchell before he could speak.

"Cal. Good to see you. And you must be Amy." The minister turned and extended his hand. At Amy's quizzical look, he smiled. "News of strangers travels fast in this part of the country. Though I hope you won't be a stranger for long."

She returned his smile. "Thank you."

He squeezed her hand, then turned back to Cal. "Are you staying long?"

"Just a couple more days."

"Too bad. I was hoping you'd have time to stop in and see Walter Thompson."

Cal frowned. Walter was one of the hardest-working, most well-respected men in the community. He'd run a local trout farm for as long as Cal could remember and was always the first to offer a hand when his neighbors needed help. "Something wrong?"

"I think he could use some good legal advice. Or at least someone to point him to some good legal advice. There's a big developer planning a mall of some sort next to his property and they're putting a lot of pressure on him to sell a section of his land. He hasn't budged so far, but now they're getting pretty nasty from what I hear, digging up all sorts of obscure laws that he's supposedly violated and threatening to put him out of business. He's pretty worried. And none of the local attorneys he's contacted seems able to cope with the legal eagles at this big conglomerate."

Cal's frown deepened. "I'll put him in touch with someone who has experience dealing with corporate law firms."

"He can't afford big-city prices, you know."

"Yeah, I figured. I'll work it out."

The minister smiled. "I'm sure anything will be appreciated, Cal. Sorry to bother you with this, but I know Walter's at his wits' end." He turned back to Amy. "It was very nice to meet you. Take care, both of you. And don't be strangers."

As Reverend Mitchell walked over to talk to another couple, Amy turned to Cal. "Do you know *everybody* here?"

He gave her a troubled glance. "Pretty much."

Amy tilted her head and gazed up at him. "You're upset."

He drew a deep breath and nodded. "I don't like to see the little guy get trampled on."

"Can you do anything?"

He sighed. "Not much. Except contact someone who can deal with the big guns of a corporate law firm. But it will come at a price."

"Which Mr. Thompson can't pay."

Cal shrugged. "I might be able to call in a few favors. I'll work something out."

As they walked toward his car, Amy considered Cal's response. He probably did have connections, probably *could* hook the man up with a good attorney who might discount his fees as a favor. But they would most likely still be more than the man could afford. And Amy suddenly had a feeling she knew who would pay the difference. The evidence was clear. Cal lived simply, and well below his means. The director at Saint Vincent's had implied that Cal contributed more than time to the boys' center. Amanda had said that he took good care of her and his father. It wasn't too hard to figure out who would come to Walter Thompson's aid, though the man would probably never realize it. Because Cal's generosity would be quiet, unobtrusive and anonymous.

Amy shook her head. She might still be puzzling over why the Lord had brought the two of them together, but one thing was clear. She'd never met anyone like Cal before. And she suddenly had a feeling that she never would again.

Chapter Eleven

❧

"So when are you going to put that forestry degree to use?"

Leave it to Doug Howell to ask the tough questions, Cal thought ruefully as the two men walked through the field next to Gram's cabin. Though Doug was several years older than Cal, they'd been fast friends since childhood, and he was one of the few people Cal had confided in about his extracurricular study. A head ranger for the National Parks Service, Doug shared Cal's love of the outdoors. So Cal had known Doug would understand his desire to study forestry. He'd also known that his friend would eventually raise this question.

The two men paused at the edge of the field, and Cal rested his forearms on the split-rail fence as he gazed out over the meadow. The midafternoon sun felt pleasantly warm on his back, easing the sudden tension in his shoulders. But it didn't make Doug's question any easier to answer.

"I never said I was."

"You didn't have to."

Cal turned to him, his mouth lifting wryly at one corner. "You know me too well."

Doug shrugged. "We've been friends a long time. I know how you feel about this place. What I *don't* know is how you've survived in that concrete jungle all these years."

Cal sighed and stared into the distance. "Neither do I. But I've built a life there now, and a career. It gets harder and harder to walk away."

"I'm sure it does. Success can be addictive."

Cal frowned and turned to his friend. "You know better than that."

Doug studied him shrewdly. "Then tell me what holds you to the city."

Cal considered the question, then carefully formed his answer, putting into words what, until now, had only been in his heart. "Dad, for one," he said slowly. "He takes such pride in my success, and he'd be tremendously disappointed if I threw my career away. Then there's the guilt. I'm not always successful in my work, but I win often enough to feel that I'm contributing *something* to the cause of justice. After all my years of training and experience, it seems wrong somehow not to put that to good use. And frankly, I'm not sure I want to give up law. Despite the frustration, I get a lot of satisfaction out of helping people who really need someone on their side, who might otherwise get lost in the legal system. And yet..." He sighed and raked his fingers through his hair. "I want to come home, Doug. I don't like the city. I never have, and it hasn't grown on me over the years. This is where I belong.''

"Then come home.''

"You make it sound so simple.''

"It can be. It's your life, Cal. And if this is where you want to spend it, come back.''

"And do what?''

Doug rested one elbow on the fence and angled toward Cal. "I'll have a part-time ranger slot opening up in about three months.''

Cal shot him a surprised look. "Are you offering me the job?''

Doug shrugged. "There'd be a lot of paperwork to fill out, of course. But you certainly have the credentials.''

"What about my law career?''

"Why can't you do both? We could use an attorney with your skills and experience around here.''

Cal frowned, jolted by Doug's suggestion. His friend was right about the need for good legal counsel in the area. Walter Thompson's situation was clear evidence of that. But the idea of splitting his time between two careers—he'd never even considered that before. Yet it was like a beam of light breaking through the clouds after a storm, illuminating a dreary world and filling it with the promise of brighter days ahead.

"You might be on to something, Doug," he acknowledged as the idea took hold, sending a surge of excitement through him.

"Seems like a logical solution to me. You'd still be using those legal skills you spent so many years honing, only you'd be helping your own people. And you'd have the chance to share your knowledge and love of nature with those poor city folks who have to squeeze their visits to God's country into a week or two of vacation.''

Cal shook his head. ''I should have talked to you a long time ago. I've been wrestling with this for months.''

''Us mountain folk have a few good ideas now and then,'' Doug teased.

Cal grinned. ''More than a few. I don't know why this option never occurred to me before. It was always either/or in my mind. But this is definitely worth some thought.''

''It's still a big decision, though,'' Doug pointed out. ''You'd be giving up a lot.''

''A lot of things that don't matter to me, anyway,'' Cal countered.

''And how would your friend feel about it?'' Doug nodded toward the distant porch where Amy and Gram sat.

Cal frowned. ''That's part of what I have to think about.''

It was funny, Cal reflected, as he turned once more to stare out over the meadow. He'd been praying for guidance on this decision. And the Lord had come through. But He'd thrown in a complication. Namely, Amy. A few weeks ago, the thought that she might even *consider* leaving the city or her present job to live in the mountains would have seemed ludicrous. And yet, as he'd come to know her, he'd begun to believe that at heart they weren't quite as different as they'd first seemed. Though their lifestyles were poles apart, their values were compatible. And she *had* expressed some dissatisfaction with her present job. So maybe, given time, she would consider rethinking her priorities. Especially if she happened to fall in love with him.

Cal prayed that she would do exactly that. Because one thing had become very clear to him on this trip. He was in love with her. And he couldn't imagine spending the rest of his life without her.

Amy watched the two men at the far end of the field with a vague and troubling sense of unease. When Cal had introduced Doug Howell to her as a childhood friend, it was her suggestion that the two men take a walk through the field. Now, for some strange reason, she wasn't so sure that had been wise.

"I remember those two boys as youngsters," Gram said from her rocking chair on the porch, reclaiming Amy's attention. "They sure were pals. Couldn't find one without the other. I think they've hiked every inch of the national park. I really can't say which one loved the mountains more."

Gram's comments did nothing to ease Amy's odd sense of trepidation, so she changed the subject.

"I enjoyed your solo in church this morning, Amanda. You have a beautiful voice."

The older woman brushed aside the comment, though she was clearly flattered. "Can't claim any credit for that. The Lord blessed me with it. So I return the favor by using it to honor Him. I've been

singing in the church choir since I was fourteen—
more than sixty years now, believe it or not.''

"When I commented to Cal that you could have
been a professional singer, he told me to ask you
about it. Sounds like there's an interesting story
there.''

Amanda smiled. ''My, that's a long time ago. Are
you sure you want to hear ancient history?''

"Absolutely.''

Amanda gazed out at the meadow, her eyes focused
not on the misty mountains, but on the past. ''Let's
see, I was about twenty-five, I guess. We had a visitor
at church one Sunday, a record producer from Nashville on vacation in the mountains. I did a solo that
day, and he came up to me after the service and
handed me his card, said he'd like me to come to
Nashville and make a test record. 'Course I had a
husband and baby to think about. Cal's father was
just five or six at the time. But I must say I was
flattered.''

"Did you go?''

"I turned him down at first. But Warren—my husband—could tell it was eating at me. So finally he
said to call the man and go do the test. Told me I
needed to see it through, check out the opportunity,
or I'd always wonder where it might have led. So I
did.''

She paused for a moment, and Amy leaned forward. ''What happened?''

"Well, I went on down to Nashville and made the
record. I guess I was there four or five days. It surely
was an exciting time, I remember that, what with see-

ing the studio and hobnobbing with musicians and staying in a fancy hotel. Then I came home and waited. And about two weeks later the man called me, said he'd played the record for a number of people, and they thought I had great potential. Offered me a recording contract."

"No kidding! What did you do?"

"I turned it down."

Amy stared at her. "But why? You could have been a star!"

"It was a funny thing," Amanda reflected. "After I went to Nashville and had a little exposure to the music world, I sort of got it out of my system. The contract offer gave me a lot of satisfaction, told me that someone who knew music thought I was good enough to make it, and that was enough. Because during those two weeks while I waited to hear back, I had a chance to look around here and evaluate what I really wanted out of my life. If I signed that contract, I'd be on the road a lot, away from my family and my mountains, for weeks and months on end. I didn't want that."

"But you could have been rich and famous," Amy protested.

Amanda shrugged. "I was already rich in all the ways that counted. I had people to love, and who loved me. I lived in one of the most beautiful places in God's creation. And I had my faith. As for fame— that's fleeting. I preferred to put my energies into things that last."

Amy digested that for a moment. "And you never had any regrets?" she pressed.

"Not a one," the older woman declared.

"I envy you," Amy said quietly.

"Why is that?"

"You seem so…content with your life. And happy with your choices."

"You sound as if you aren't."

Amy sighed. "I'm beginning to wonder."

"Nothing wrong with wondering. And you're too young for regrets. So if there's anything you want to change in your life, you still have plenty of time."

As Amy glanced toward the field where Cal and Doug stood, she pondered Amanda's words. She supposed she did still have the time to make changes. But did she have the courage?

"Amy?" Cal leaned back in his chair and smiled. "It's good to hear your voice."

"You just heard it last night," she teased, even as a flush of pleasure tinged her cheeks at the warmth in his tone. Though they'd spent every possible free minute together since their return from the mountains, it never seemed enough.

"That was ten hours ago. And besides, good-night calls aren't cutting it anymore. I need more than a voice at the end of the day, sweetheart."

The husky, intimate cadence in his voice sent a sweet shiver of delight up her spine. "I agree. This work thing is starting to get old. Either you're tied up late or I am. We've got to do something about this."

"Any suggestions?"

"How about a trip back to the mountains?"

Cal's eyebrows rose in surprise. "We were just there six weeks ago."

"Can't you get away?"

"Probably. For a couple of days, anyway. What brought this up?"

"Honestly? Work. I'd like to do a piece on Amanda's craft co-op. I think it has great human-interest potential. And it would give me a chance to focus some attention on the economic problems in Appalachia. Not to mention focusing some attention on us. Do you think she'd go along with the idea?"

Cal fought down his disappointment. For a moment he'd thought her suggestion for the trip had been motivated not only by a desire for the two of them to have some time together, but by a growing love for the mountains. She'd talked glowingly about the Smokies in the weeks since their return, but clearly he'd read too much into those comments.

"Cal? Are you still there?"

"Yeah. I think we could convince Gram. When would you like to go?"

"Well, once she says okay, I have to sell the idea to the station. But the Saint Vincent's piece went over really well, so I don't think I'll have any trouble. Probably in a couple of weeks."

"Okay. I'll give her a call. Any chance of getting together for dinner tonight?"

Amy glanced at her calendar and noted the late-afternoon meeting she'd scheduled with one of the producers for an upcoming series. It was sure to run into the early evening. She bit her lip and considered her options: Sit through a long meeting, or share dinner—and hopefully some kisses—with Cal. Put that way, it was no contest. She reached over and crossed out the meeting.

"That's the best offer I've had all day," she replied with a smile. "Just pick the time and place."

Cal propped one shoulder against the door frame of the co-op, shoved his hands into his pockets and crossed one ankle over the other as he watched Amy wrap up the last bit of filming for the story. Though the trip had turned out to be far more work than play, he had nevertheless been impressed once again by her professionalism, intensity and thoroughness. She was extraordinarily talented, and he had no doubt that, given time, she would reach all of her career goals. The network slot she craved was a very real possibility in her future.

Cal fingered the ring box in his pocket and frowned. Was he wrong to ask her to give up her dreams? Or at the very least, dramatically modify them? Because that's what being his wife would entail. And yet, during the two months since their first visit to the mountains, it had become clear to him that Amy's priorities were shifting. He wasn't sure if she was even aware of it yet, but he'd seen enough evidence to validate his theory. She'd begun to work more normal hours. She'd traded in her car, as she said she did every three years, but she'd exchanged her sporty model for a practical four-door compact sedan. She now seemed perfectly content to spend quiet evenings with him, cuddled up on the couch eating popcorn and watching old movies, instead of hitting the hot nightspots. Okay, so it was all circumstantial evidence. But it was also compelling. She was already altering her lifestyle, and he'd begun to hope that maybe, just maybe, she'd consider other career options, as well, such as freelancing, which would allow her to use her exceptional reporting talents and still live in the mountains. That was what he was praying for, anyway.

He transferred his gaze to his father, who had come to watch the filming and was now sitting quietly off to one side. That was the next hurdle, Cal thought, his stomach churning. But Cal had taken Reverend Mitchell's sermon about decisions, as well as Doug Howell's suggestion, to heart and had made the only choice that would allow him to be true to himself. He was going to return to the mountains. Doug already knew, and Cal had spent the last couple of weeks looking into office space in nearby Maryville in anticipation of setting up a local practice. On this trip, while Amy had been busy working, he'd also found the land he wanted to buy and build on—assuming Amy liked it, as well. He planned to show it to her later in the day—then ask her to be his wife on the very spot he planned to build the cabin they would share. But first, he wanted to break the news of his career change to his father. Though he knew the older man would be disappointed, he also knew in his heart it was the right thing for him to do.

"Okay, Steve, that should do it."

The cameraman turned off his lights and hefted the camera from his shoulder. "Looks like another good piece, Amy."

"Thanks. Are you heading back this afternoon?"

"Yep. What about you?"

"Tomorrow. I have a few things here to attend to first." She glanced toward Cal, whose lazy smile brought a flush to her cheeks.

As Steve put away his equipment, Cal pushed away from the door frame and strolled toward her. She watched him approach, her pulse accelerating at the banked fire in his eyes.

"So am I finally going to get you to myself for a while?" he asked huskily when he came up beside her.

She gave him a guilty look. "I'm sorry, Cal. I didn't expect it to take quite this long."

"I'm not complaining. Yet."

She smiled. "Message received. My evening is yours."

"Good. Because there's something I want to show you."

She tilted her head and gazed at him curiously. "What?"

He reached over and touched the tip of her nose with his finger. "Take off your reporter hat. No more questions for now. It's a surprise. Didn't you tell me once you liked surprises?"

"I believe I did."

"I rest my case."

"Okay, Amy, I'm taking off." Steve came up beside them. "See you back at the studio."

"Right. Have a safe trip."

As the cameraman left, Amanda appeared from the back room, her eyes sparkling with excitement. "My, wasn't that fun! I hope everything went the way you wanted,'' she said to Amy.

"Perfect. I think it will be a great story."

"Are we ready to head home?" Cal asked.

Amanda nodded. "Soon as we find your dad."

Cal glanced toward the empty chair where his father had been sitting. "He was over there a few minutes ago. I'll round him up and meet you ladies outside."

"I expect you're tired," Amanda commented as she and Amy exited. "All that running around doing interviews, not to mention all the research you did before you came here. Even I learned something about the economy of Appalachia, and I've lived here all my life."

Amy grinned. "Cal says I never do anything halfway. I guess he's right."

"There's a lot to be said for... Cal, what is it?"

At the alarm in Amanda's voice, Amy turned back toward the door. Cal stood on the threshold, his face pale and tight with tension. There was fear in his eyes, and Amy's stomach plummeted to her toes.

"I think dad's having a heart attack. Call 911." Without giving either woman time to respond, he turned on his heel and disappeared back inside.

"Dear Lord," Amanda whispered, automatically moving toward the door. Amy followed, dumping her shoulder tote on a chair before going in search of Cal and his father. She found them in the back hall. The older man was sitting on the floor clutching his left arm, his back against the wall. His face was gray and creased with pain, and he was sweating profusely. Cal was down on his haunches beside him, holding his father's hand.

"Everything will be okay, Dad. Just try to relax."

Amy knelt beside them and put her hand on Cal's shoulder. "Can I do anything?" she asked quietly.

"Just pray," he said tightly, his gaze never leaving his father's face.

Amanda joined them a few moments later, and the three of them kept a silent, agonizing vigil. It seemed to take hours before the distant sound of sirens signaled the approach of help. Though Amy knew the wait had been less than fifteen minutes, she also knew every second counted with a heart attack. And so she did as Cal asked—she prayed that the emergency crew would arrive in time to keep the damage to a minimum.

The paramedics went into action immediately, quickly confirming Cal's diagnosis. When they whisked the older man off in an ambulance a few minutes later, Cal accompanied them while Amy and Amanda followed in his car. The older woman was clearly distraught, and Amy wished she could think of something comforting to say. But until they knew more, any hope she offered would be just that—hope, with no basis in fact. And so she remained silent, continuing her prayers—as she knew Amanda was doing.

Cal was in the hospital waiting room when they arrived, and he answered their question before they could ask.

"No word yet. The nurse said they'd let us know something as soon as they can." His gaze rested on

Gram, and he frowned. For the first time in his memory, she actually looked her age. Deep lines were etched in her face, and she seemed old and frail. He put his arm around her shoulders and guided her to a chair. "Sit down, Gram," he said gently. "I'll get you some tea."

"I'm fine," she protested shakily. "Don't bother with me."

"I saw a snack shop down the hall," Amy said quietly to Cal. "I'll get the tea. Do you want coffee?"

He nodded, but as she turned to go, he restrained her with a hand on her arm. She glanced back, and for a moment their gazes connected—as did their hearts. "I'm glad you're here," he said softly. And she knew he meant not just here, in this hospital waiting room, but here, in his life.

Her throat constricted with emotion and she laid her hand over his. "So am I."

When she returned a few minutes later, the questioning look she directed at him was met with a shake of his head, and she slipped into the seat beside him and reached for his hand. He gripped it fiercely, like a lifeline, as they kept their silent, tense vigil.

It was almost an hour later—an hour that seemed like an eternity—before a doctor finally stepped into the waiting room and looked in their direction.

"Are you the family of Mr. Richards?"

They were on their feet instantly. "Yes," Cal replied, his grip tightening on Amy's hand.

The man walked toward them. "I'm Dr. Douglas. Let me put your minds at ease right away. I think Mr. Richards will make a good recovery."

"Thank God!" murmured Amanda fervently. Though Cal made no comment, Amy could feel the sudden release of tension in his muscles, and she squeezed his hand.

"Let's sit down for a moment, shall we?" the doctor suggested.

When they complied, the doctor opened a folder and withdrew several pieces of film. He walked them through the images, explaining the extent of the heart damage and the good prognosis for recovery.

"Your father is in excellent physical condition, and fortunately the damage is minimal. With therapy and common sense, he should do very well," he concluded as he slipped the film back inside the folder. "We'll watch him closely for a few days just to be sure, but I don't expect any complications."

"Can we see him?" Amanda asked.

"We're moving him to intensive care right now. I'll have the nurse come get you as soon as he's settled." At their looks of alarm, he raised his hand reassuringly. "Cardiac intensive care is standard procedure for at least twenty-four hours after a heart attack. And don't be alarmed by all the equipment and monitors. We just want to play it safe. Please trust me on this. I believe in being honest, and I often have to deliver a prognosis that's much more grim. In this case, I'm very hopeful about recovery."

He stood, and they followed suit.

"Thank you, Doctor," Cal said.

"Glad we could help."

As they watched him leave, Amy's vibrating pager

went off, and she removed it from her belt to glance at the message.

"Work?"

She responded to Cal's question with a distracted nod. "I need to call in. There are some phones by the coffee shop. I'll be back in a couple of minutes."

"Take your time."

Only when Amy reached up to punch the numbers in the phone did she realize how badly shaken she was by the events that had transpired over the past couple of hours. Her fingers were trembling, her legs suddenly felt unsteady and a tension headache pulsated in her temples. She was *not* in the mood to talk about work.

"Newsroom."

"Jarrod? Amy Winter. I got your message. What's up?" Though she tried for a businesslike tone, she couldn't control the tremor that ran through her voice.

"Where are you?"

The news editor was certainly living up to his reputation for not mincing words, Amy thought in irritation. "I'm still in the Smokies."

"How quickly can you get back?"

She frowned. "Why?"

"Remember those rumors that were going around a few months ago about one certain very influential and powerful alderman with national political aspirations who supposedly had mob connections? Looks like it was more than rumor. We've got a hot tip that a major scandal is about to break, possibly as early as first thing in the morning. Could result in criminal charges. We want you here to cover the story."

Amy knew she should be flattered to be singled out for such a high-profile story. She knew that it could move her up another rung or two on the career ladder. She knew that she would be the envy of her colleagues for being handed such a plum assignment.

She also knew she didn't want to go back. She wanted—needed—to be here with Cal. *For* Cal.

It was decision time. And she knew the choice she was about to make wasn't going to sit well with the news editor. She drew a deep breath and willed the pounding of her heart to subside.

"There's a complication here, Jarrod," she said as evenly as she could.

The silence on the other end of the line communicated his reaction more eloquently than words. It was the first time in her career that she hadn't responded by dropping everything when the station said "Jump," and Jarrod was clearly shocked.

When he finally spoke, his voice was cautious. "What do you mean?"

Amy played with the phone cord. "A friend's father just had a heart attack. I'm at the hospital now, in fact. I need to stay a couple more days. I have plenty of vacation saved up."

"Is this friend the guy who answered the phone at your apartment after you got hurt covering the hostage story?"

She hesitated, surprised by the question. "As a matter of fact, yes."

"Look, Amy, romances come and go," Jarrod said impatiently. "You're building a career here. I think you need to get your priorities straight."

She took a deep breath. "So do I."

"So are you coming back?"

"No."

She cringed at his crude expletive. "Fine. Stay in the mountains. But don't expect us to call you first the next time a great story comes along."

The bang on the other end abruptly ended their conversation, and she slowly replaced the receiver. Jarrod might be a good news editor, but his interpersonal skills could definitely use some polishing, she concluded as she took a deep, steadying breath. Yet he'd put into words what she'd always known instinctively. If she wanted to get ahead in this business, the job had to come first. That was the expectation. And until now she'd always accepted it. Somehow, though, in the face of what had transpired in the past few hours, the "job first" philosophy had a hollow ring.

As she made her way back to the waiting room, she reflected again on Reverend Mitchell's sermon about choices. She'd made a career choice once, a long time ago, when she'd set her sights on a network feature slot. She'd made a choice just now, one that could cost her dearly. And yet, it felt right. Because over the past few months she had learned something. Success was important to her. But so was love. And if making the two compatible meant revising her definition of success, maybe that was okay. Maybe a job that didn't allow her to put the people she loved first wasn't worth having. After all, Atlanta was a big city. There had to be other options.

For the first time in a long while, Amy didn't have

a clear vision of what her future held. It was an unsettling—and unwelcome—feeling. And yet, in her
heart she knew that it was time to face some of the
questions that Cal's presence in her life had raised.
The choices ahead of her weren't necessarily going
to be easy, she realized. But supported by Cal's love,
and guided by her renewed faith, she had the courage
to hope for a tomorrow that was even better than the
one she'd so carefully planned.

Chapter Twelve

Cal watched Amy's Atlanta-bound plane disappear into the clouds, then turned and walked wearily back to his car. The last two days were a blur of images in his sleep-starved brain—his father's face, pale against the stark white of the hospital sheets; the impersonal beeping and blinking of high-tech health care, a sharp contrast to the folksy print of a country doctor that he'd stared at for hours on end in the waiting room between visits to the cardiac intensive-care unit; and Amy, always close by, her quiet presence a balm on his tattered nerves.

A wave of tenderness swept over him as he recalled her concerned eyes, soft with sympathy and shared pain, which had made him feel less alone and afraid; her delicate hand entwined with his, the touch of her slender fingers giving him strength; her tired face, relaxed in sleep when she'd drifted off during their middle-of-the-night vigils, the shadows under her eyes offering a mute testament to her empathy and worry. He'd tried to convince her to go home with Gram and get some rest, but she had categorically refused. Her steadfast presence had meant more to him than he could ever say—and reaffirmed for him how much he wanted her to be a permanent part of his life.

Unfortunately, he'd had no opportunity to tell her that, he thought ruefully, fingering the small, square box in his pocket. The ring that he had hoped she would now be wearing still lay nestled on its velvet cushion. But not for long, he resolved. His first priority when he returned to Atlanta was to put the ring where it belonged—on the third finger of her left hand.

The timing on his other piece of unfinished business—breaking the news about his career shift to his father—was less clear. As he parked in the hospital lot and made his way to the older man's room—a regular room now, not cardiac intensive care, thank God—he prayed for guidance on how and when to broach the subject.

When he reached the doorway, he paused to study his father, whose gaze was fixed on something outside the window. The lines of pain in his face had eased, and his color was much better, Cal noted with relief. He seemed to be resting comfortably, though it was odd to see him in a prone position. While his father had always moved at a slower, more methodical pace than Gram, he was always busy doing something—usually for other people. Only in recent years had he allowed himself the luxury of time for himself, to read or go for walks or take in an occasional movie or sports event. Through all of Cal's growing-up years, his father had always been a quiet, dependable figure who put his family above all else. Only as an adult had Cal come to fully appreciate the extent of the sacrifices his father had made to give his only son a good education and a better life.

As if sensing his presence, the older man turned and smiled. "Hello, Cal."

Cal swallowed past the lump in this throat. "Hi, Dad."

"Amy get off okay?"

"She's almost back to Atlanta by now." Cal moved toward the bed and dropped into the chair beside it, stretching his long legs out in front of him.

"Nice girl."

"Yeah."

"You look tired, son."

"It's been a tough few days."

"I'm sure sorry to put you and your grandmother through all this."

"It's not your fault, Dad."

The older man sighed. "I suppose not. But I don't like just lying around. I have things to do."

"They'll wait. The most important thing you can do right now is rest."

"Can't say that's ever appealed to me much. I like to keep busy. But I guess the Lord has His reasons for things." He hesitated and glanced down, picking at the white blanket that covered his slight form, a frown creasing his brow. When he spoke again, he seemed to be choosing his words carefully. "Fact is, I've had a lot of time to think during the past few days. About things I've put off coming to terms with for too long. I'm grateful that I came through this so well, but it sure was a wake-up call. Reminded me I had some unfinished business."

Cal looked at him curiously. "What do you mean?"

The older man sighed. "I realized something, lying here in this hospital, Cal. I'm a selfish man."

Cal frowned and straightened up. "That's ridiculous, Dad. You're one of the most *unselfish* people I know. All those years you sacrificed for me, put my future above everything... How can you say that?"

"Because it's true. I *am* selfish, and it's been weighing heavily on my mind. I should have said something to you years ago, but I just couldn't get the words out. Took a heart attack for me to realize how wrong I've been, and to be grateful for having a second chance to make things right."

"What are you talking about?"

The older man fixed his gaze on Cal and took a deep breath. "Here it is in a nutshell, son. I always knew you loved the mountains. Loved them in a way I never did. You're like your grandmother, born with the mountain mist in your veins. I could see the joy in your eyes when you came back, and the pain every time you had to leave. But I ignored it. I wanted you to have a better life, and in my mind that meant a good job in the city. And you've done me proud on that score, son. So proud that I didn't want to give up bragging rights. And too proud to do the right thing. Which is to tell you that I love you, and that if your idea of success is different than mine, you need to follow your heart and do what's right for you without worrying about disappointing me. I don't want you to look back at the end of your life and discover that you've lived someone else's dream. You're a fine man, Cal, and you deserve to follow your own dream, whatever that is. Because more than anything else, I want you to be happy."

Cal stared at his father, his vision blurring as his eyes slowly misted with tears. He'd always loved and admired the man who'd given him life, but now his father had given him the most precious gift of all. Freedom. Freedom to pursue his own vision of happiness without worrying about disappointing the man who meant so much to him. He felt as if a great burden had been lifted from his shoulders.

"I stand by what I said earlier, Dad," Cal said in a choked voice. "You're still the most unselfish man I've ever met."

His father's own eyes looked suspiciously moist as he reached over and clasped Cal's hand. "I'm glad you still feel that way, son. But I should have done this years ago."

"I've had a good career in Atlanta, Dad. I've learned a lot. The time wasn't wasted."

"But you're coming home now, aren't you?" It was more statement than question.

Cal nodded slowly. "Yes. As a matter of fact, I'd already made that decision. I was just waiting for the right time to tell you."

His father smiled gently. "I guess my timing was pretty good, then. Can I ask you something else?"

"Of course."

"I don't mean to pry, but Amy sure is a nice girl, and I wondered... Will you be coming back alone?"

A hopeful smile touched the corners of Cal's mouth and his eyes grew tender. "Not if I can help it, Dad."

As the doorbell rang, Amy glanced at the clock and smiled. Seven o'clock on the dot. Punctuality was just one of Cal's many admirable qualities, as well as a reflection of the solid dependability she had come to count on in him.

She glanced in the mirror and adjusted a stray strand of hair, smoothed down her pencil-slim black skirt and took a deep breath. Though Cal had returned from the mountains two days ago and they'd spoken frequently by phone, there'd been no opportunity to get together. And for her, like Cal, phone conversations just weren't cutting it anymore.

She opened the door eagerly, but before she could say a word she found herself pulled into his arms as his lips hungrily claimed hers. Though momentarily surprised by his ardent greeting, she didn't object. She felt need in his kiss, as well as fire, and she returned it fully. When he at last lifted his head, he kept his arms looped around her waist and gave her a smoky, intimate smile.

"Hi," he said huskily.

"Hi, yourself," she replied breathlessly. "I think I like this greeting much better than a mere 'hello.'"

He chuckled. "Sorry. I got a little carried away. In case you haven't figured it out, I missed you."

Her gaze softened. "I missed you, too, Cal. How's your dad?"

"Improving every day. But it will take time."

She reached up and caressed his weary face. "You look exhausted."

He passed off her comment with a shrug. "I've been more tired. Like when I was cramming for the bar exam. But I was younger then, too," he added, his lips tipping up into a rueful grin.

Amy stepped out of his arms and took his hand. "Come on in. I have some wine chilling, and you look like you could use some. I thought we might have a glass before we went to dinner."

"That sounds great."

By the time Amy returned with two glasses, Cal was settled comfortably on the couch. A white envelope lay on the glass-topped coffee table, and she looked at him curiously as she handed him a glass and sat beside him.

"What's that?"

He didn't answer immediately. Instead, he took a slow sip of his wine, willing his pulse and respiration to behave. Now that the moment was upon him, he was filled with doubts. So much of his future depended on what transpired in this room in the next few minutes, and he was suddenly afraid. Afraid to ask the question. Afraid to hear the answer. Afraid that all along he'd been reading more into Amy's feelings than was actually there. But he'd come too far now to let fear stop him, so he took a deep breath, placed his wineglass carefully on the table and picked up the envelope.

"Pictures. I wanted to show you this place in person, but the best-laid plans and all that…"

As he opened the envelope, Amy suddenly found her own pulse skyrocketing. Cal was not a man who got rattled easily, but he was definitely nervous now—and doing his best to hide it. She could sense it in the almost imperceptible tremor that ran through his hand, in the way his Adam's apple bobbed convulsively when he swallowed, in the tense line of his jaw. Something big was in the wind.

Cal withdrew several photos from the envelope and handed them to her. "I found this spot while you were filming the story with Gram. Take a look."

Amy slowly examined the four photos, her own hands none too steady. They were all shots of the same beautiful, serene spot, taken from different angles. She paused on the last one, a meadow backed by misty mountains, then glanced up at Cal.

"This is a lovely place, Cal. Is there something special about it, other than its beauty?"

Cal took a deep breath and nodded slowly. "I'd like to buy it. Build a cabin that looks out directly on that view." He nodded toward the photograph in her hand.

Amy glanced back down at the picture. "It would make a great weekend getaway."

He cleared his throat. "Actually, Amy, I'm thinking of making it a permanent getaway."

She sent him a startled gaze. "What do you mean?"

Cal reached into the pocket of his jacket and withdrew a small jeweler's box. Amy's gaze dropped to the square package, then returned to his as her heart stopped, then raced on.

"I wanted to do this right there," he said, again nodding toward the photo, "on the spot where I'd like to build a cabin. I wanted to stand with you under the setting sun, in the midst of God's beautiful creation, and ask you to spend the rest of your life with me. But this will have to do, because I can't wait any longer."

He reached over and took her hand, his intense gaze locked on hers. "If someone had told me the day we met that someday I'd ask you to marry me, I would have thought they were crazy," he admitted, his voice slightly unsteady. "But I think we've both discovered over the past few months that we have a lot more in common than either of us expected. And somewhere along the way I fell in love with you. With your energy and compassion and commitment and sense of humor—all the things that make you who you are. I want to spend the rest of my life listening to your laughter, waking up next to you, watching your eyes glow with passion and enthusiasm and joy and all the other emotions that have enriched my life so much these past few months. I want to build a future with you, Amy. A future that counts for more than dollars or prestige or power, and that will leave a lasting legacy of love for our children and their children."

He paused and drew a deep breath. "I love you, Amy. And I want to share the rest of my life with you. Would you do me the honor of becoming my wife?"

Amy stared at him in shock. Not because of the proposal. She'd known for some time that they were heading in this direction. Cal had made his feelings for her clear, and she had reciprocated. Over the past several months she had come to accept—and love—him for who he was: a man who had the opportunity for power and wealth, but who found no inherent value in those things. A man who gave generously, and without recognition, to others. A man of both strength and gentleness, who had an infinite capacity to love.

Amy had also learned much from Cal. Thanks to him, she had begun to realign her own priorities, had begun to set some limits on the sacrifices she was willing to make to advance her career. And she had come to realize that she could be content to share a simple life with this very special man, who made her rich in ways that couldn't be measured in dollars and cents. She was more than willing to change her lifestyle.

But Cal wasn't asking her to change her lifestyle. He was asking her to change her *life*. Dramatically. It was one thing to put career in second place and live a simpler life in the city, but to give up her career entirely and move to the mountains—it was too much. Though she was prepared to modify her dreams to accommodate him, she couldn't give them up entirely. Not after all the years she'd spent honing her skills. She'd worked too hard and come too far to just walk away.

Cal saw the emotions sweep over Amy's face—first shock, followed in succession by confusion, disbelief, hurt and, finally, resistance. His gut clenched, and he suddenly found it difficult to breathe. Apparently his closing argument had been unconvincing, though he'd labored over it far longer than any he'd ever prepared for the courtroom. As he watched, her eyes slowly filled with tears, and his throat tightened painfully. He sensed her closing down, slipping away, and he felt powerless to stop it.

Slowly he reached over and gently touched her cheek. "I can't say this is the reaction I was praying for," he admitted, his voice catching. "I always hoped, whenever I finally proposed to the woman I loved, that she'd be happy, not sad."

"Oh, Cal." Amy's voice was choked, as well. "I—I am happy. And honored. But I had no idea you were thinking about making such a radical change in your life. Why didn't you say something about this sooner? At least give me a clue about what you were considering?"

It was a valid question. And she deserved an honest answer. "For one thing, I wasn't sure myself," he said slowly. "I've been struggling with this for a long time. Years, actually. I've never felt at home in the city, Amy. I've tried to make it work, but the only place I'm really happy is in the mountains. I put off this decision longer than I should have, because I didn't want to disappoint Dad. And then, just when I finally got to the point of deciding that I had to follow my heart, you came along. I know I should have shared this with you sooner, but I was afraid of what it would mean to us. I guess I hoped that if I waited long enough, if we fell in love, we'd find a way to make this work."

"But how?" she asked helplessly. "What would I do? And what about *your* career?"

"I'll still practice law part-time. And I've been offered a job with the National Parks Service as a ranger. I know it doesn't have the prestige of law, but it's what I've always wanted to do. And you've said more than once that you're not altogether happy with your job, that you'd like to find a way to do more feature and issues reporting. I thought you might be open to exploring that."

Amy stared at him incredulously. "In the mountains? My contacts are all here, Cal. In this business, the 'out of sight, out of mind' adage really holds true."

"I'm sure we can find a way to make this work, Amy." There was a pleading tone in his voice, but he didn't care. "I'd stay in the city if I could, but I feel like I'm dying a little more each day in this concrete jungle. And I can't live someone else's dream any longer."

"Yet you want me to live yours."

Her blunt comment jolted him, and he frowned. "That's not true."

"Yes, it is. You're asking me to give up everything and follow *your* dream."

"No, I'm not. You're too good at what you do to stop doing it. I'm just asking for some compromises."

"It sounds to me like all the compromises are on my side." The hurt in her eyes had given way to anger, and her voice was taut. She rose and walked across the room, clearly agitated. When she turned to him, two bright spots of color burned in her cheeks and she wrapped her arms around herself in an almost protective gesture. "I thought I knew you pretty well, Cal. But I was wrong. You let me fall in love with you, knowing all along how I felt about my work, knowing that you were thinking of leaving the city, knowing how difficult it would be for me to continue in my profession—in any capacity—in the middle of nowhere. You weren't honest with me, and that was wrong."

He couldn't dispute her accusation. He'd always known that withholding that vital piece of information from Amy was a calculated risk, and now he realized just how serious a mistake he had made. Slowly he rose and walked toward her. Her body language clearly said "Back off," and so he stopped a couple of feet away from her.

"I'm sorry," he said quietly. "You're right. I should have shared this with you sooner. I was just so afraid of losing you."

Amy turned away, fighting to keep her tears at bay. She didn't want to cry in front of Cal, didn't want to feel his comforting arms around her. That would make it too easy to give in, to offer to make sacrifices she'd later regret.

"What if I said I'd stay here?"

His quiet voice, touched with desperation, tore at her heart, and she choked back a sob. "After telling me you're dying a little bit more in the city every day, do you really think I could live with myself if I let you do that?"

Amy walked to the window and stared out, oblivious to the city lights twinkling below. Her world was falling apart, and she saw no way to hold it together. Even if they found a way to accommodate each other's needs, the pain would remain. She felt betrayed and used and disillusioned. Love was built on trust, and Cal hadn't trusted her with the greatest secret of his heart. He hadn't shared his dreams. Amy wasn't sure if the outcome would have been any different if he'd opened up to her sooner, but at least they could have talked it through, maybe come to some understanding. As it was, he'd thrown the proposal and announcement on her all at once, linking them inexorably. The implication was clear: If you accept one, you must accept the other. And she couldn't do that.

Slowly she turned back to him. The pain in his eyes almost did her in, but she steeled herself to it, and when she spoke, her voice was surprisingly steady.

"You've made your decision, Cal. Without consulting me. You have your life set up exactly the way you want it, and I'm happy for you. But it's not the life I want. You're asking me to give up my dreams, just like your father did with you. I thought you understood how important my work is to me. You may be able to be a part-time lawyer in the mountains, but I can't be a part-time journalist, at least not doing the kind of stories I want to do. Sure, maybe I could get hired to read the news on a local station. But that's not good enough, Cal. I have more to offer than that."

Cal wanted to pull her into his arms, into a world where only they existed, unencumbered by conflicts and complications. But love didn't happen in a vacuum. And the real world wasn't going to go away.

He'd hoped their love would be strong enough to overcome their differences. But he'd been wrong. Wrong to think love could solve all problems, and wrong to expect Amy to so easily accommodate his dreams. Somehow, somewhere along the way, he realized he'd discounted her dreams. He hadn't meant to do that, and her resentment was valid. But one of them had to give, and much as he loved her, he couldn't give any more. He needed to go back to the mountains as badly as he needed air to breathe. The trouble was, he needed Amy, too.

Cal raked his fingers through his hair, silently berating himself for how badly he'd handled the whole situation. When his gaze met hers once again, it was filled with love and apology. "I know I've hurt you, Amy. I should have brought all this up a long time ago. But I was so afraid of losing you. Can we at least talk about it?"

She shook her head. "I don't think we have anything to talk about. There's no way to make this work, Cal."

He looked at her for a moment in silence, and when he spoke, his voice rang with quiet sincerity and an intensity that came right from the soul. "I love you, Amy."

At the simple, heartfelt statement, she drew a ragged breath and turned away, blinking back her tears. "Trust is part of love, Cal. So is understanding. And respect."

Cal looked at Amy's rigid back, realized just how deeply he'd hurt her and knew that there was nothing else he could do at the moment. He walked back to the coffee table and picked up the ring box, weighing it in his hand before slipping it into his pocket.

"I'll call you," he said.

"It might be better if you don't."

The finality in her tone made his stomach clench painfully. He didn't want to leave, not like this, but she was giving him no choice. Slowly he walked toward the door, hoping that she would stop him. But when he looked back, she was still turned away, her posture stiff and unyielding. It was clear to him that this was one problem he couldn't solve by himself. And so, as he let himself out, he turned to a greater power.

Lord, please help me, he prayed silently. *I love Amy. I thought her priorities were changing, that she could be happy in the mountains, but obviously I was wrong. Maybe she can only be happy here, in the city, working in that dog-eat-dog business. But I can't. And I've sacrificed my own needs for so long. Do I have to continue to do that in order to have the woman I love? And wouldn't I eventually resent her if I did? Lord, I don't want to be selfish. Please help us find a way to make this work that doesn't require either of us to give up our dreams. I know that's a large order, but I also believe that nothing is impossible with You. So please, Lord, help me find a solution. Because I don't want to lose this once-in-a-lifetime woman.*

Chapter Thirteen

Amy stared at the photo of the mountain meadow, as she did most mornings while she sipped her tea. It would be pretty there this time of year, she reflected wistfully, with the leaves touched by the russet tones of autumn and the sky most likely a clear, cobalt blue. Almost three months had elapsed since she'd last seen Cal. Three long, lonely months filled with questions and doubts. Over and over she had asked herself if she'd been wrong to turn down his proposal. And always her heart said yes. Called her a fool. Berated her for throwing away the gift of such a special man's love. But the yearnings of her heart were overridden by the strident voice of pride, which wouldn't let her forget his seemingly cavalier dismissal of her dreams. And by logic, which told her that after investing so much time and energy in her career, she couldn't change course midstream. And by hurt. Cal's unwillingness to trust her with his own dreams still stung.

And finally by fear. Fear that kept her clinging tightly to the lifeline of her job, which, as she knew, played far too large a role in helping define her life and give it value.

Amy fingered the photo, then picked up the only other physical evidence of Cal's presence in her life—the card that had been attached to the flowers he'd sent after their first date. Four photos and a tiny florist card. That was it. There were no other lingering reminders of Cal in her life.

Except for the memories.

Ah, the memories. Of their initial, unfriendly meeting on the courthouse steps. Of their first "date," strained in the beginning, then cordial. Of their warm and friendly encounter at Saint Vincent's. Of her emergency room visit, and Cal's touching care and concern. Of their trip to the mountains, when they had at last acknowledged their growing feelings for each other. Of the subsequent development of their romance and the glow it had added to her life. And finally, of their painful and heart-wrenching breakup.

Amy sighed and glanced at the phone, knowing that she had only to pick up the receiver and dial Cal's number to bridge the impasse between them. He'd told her that on one of the many messages he'd left, his mellow voice playing havoc with her tattered emotions. "I'm here if you ever change your mind, Amy," he'd said. "I still love you. I always will. But I won't force the issue. I only want you to come if it's what you want."

His calls had tapered off lately, and she couldn't

blame him for cutting back, especially given her total lack of response. He'd made his position clear, laid his feelings on the table for her to accept or reject, and now the ball was in her court.

Trouble was, she didn't know what to do with it.

What she *did* know was that she'd changed over the past few months. She'd begun to find the hustle and noise and impersonal nature of the city less and less appealing. She'd begun to look at her job with an increasingly jaded eye, her earlier disillusionment fed by several less-than-plum assignments that made her realize what a fickle business the daily news game was. More than a few times, she'd found herself wishing for the quiet, serene beauty of the mountains. And always she found herself longing for Cal—for his gentle touch, his caring ways, his ability to make her laugh one moment and send her pulse skyrocketing the next.

Amy had always known that a proposal from Cal would require her to modify her lifestyle. And she'd been prepared to do that. Had, in fact, found that idea more and more appealing. She'd also been more than willing to cut back on work, even if that meant it would take her a little longer to reach her goals. What she *hadn't* been prepared to do was pack up her entire life, move to the mountains and strike out in an entirely new career direction. That kind of change seemed far too abrupt and permanent—and it scared her.

And yet…she missed Cal. Desperately. It was as if the sun had dimmed since he'd left, casting a dark shadow on her world. She'd tried praying about the situation, but so far, no guidance had been offered. She felt in limbo, alone and confused. Even Kate hadn't been much help. Her sister had been sympathetic, of course, and supportive, but Amy knew that Kate didn't really understand. For her, love always came first, no matter the sacrifice. And maybe she was right. Maybe if love didn't come first, it wasn't strong enough to survive the test of time.

Yet she *did* love Cal, Amy cried silently. With all her heart. But couldn't she also love her work? Why did it have to be either/or? She didn't want to give up doing broadcast work that made a difference, that touched and improved people's lives. Like the Appalachia piece. Good, solid reporting that combined feature and issues work in a seamless way that increased awareness about a serious economic problem under the guise of an entertaining personality profile. In fact, that piece had been nominated for a local Emmy. It was a career coup, one she'd always yearned for, and yet she hadn't been able to work up much enthusiasm about it, even with the awards dinner now only hours away. Somehow, without Cal to share it with, the honor lost some of its luster.

With a sigh, Amy rose and emptied the dregs of her tea into the sink. Unfortunately, her doubts and confusion couldn't be so easily washed away, she thought resignedly. Why did life always present such difficult choices? Cal had suggested that the choice didn't have to be that difficult, that she could have both, but she'd denied it. Told him that a move to the mountains would require tremendous compromises on her part. But was that really true? she suddenly wondered. Certainly, it would require *changes*. But a change was only a compromise if it was done to make someone else happy. If freely chosen, it was no longer a compromise.

Amy frowned as she considered that new insight, which put a different slant on the whole situation. Maybe, if she approached it from that perspective, she might be able to find a way to work things out.

It was certainly worth some deliberation, she resolved, as she slung her purse over her shoulder and headed out the door. Because the thought of spending the rest of her life without Cal was even more scary than making a major career change.

"And the winner is…Amy Winters, for 'Appalachia: A World Apart.'"

The ballroom erupted in applause, and Amy let her breath out slowly. She'd done it! She'd actually done it! The coveted Emmy was hers. Okay, so the presenter had said her name wrong, adding an *s* to Winter. What did he know? She was just one more name on a long list to him. As she was to most of the people in the room, she thought, as she rose and made her way to the front.

Amy took the statuette, stepped to the microphone and looked out on the sea of mostly unfamiliar faces. The room was filled with strangers who didn't really care about how much this honor meant to her, she realized, who wouldn't care, in fact, if she got hit by a car while going home tonight. The people who did and would care, and the one face that meant the most to her, were absent. And without those people to share this moment with, the victory was less sweet, she acknowledged with a poignant pang.

As these realizations swept over her, she took a deep breath and forced herself to concentrate on remembering the short speech she'd prepared in case she won.

"As all of you know, the Emmy is one of the highest honors in our profession. So I'm deeply grateful to have been chosen for this award. At the same time, I'm also grateful to have the opportunity to work on stories like this, which have the potential to make life better for so many people. That's the real reward in this business. I think we often get so involved in the day-to-day reporting that we lose sight of the bigger picture, of the tremendous potential for good that our medium offers. And I think it's our responsibility to exploit that potential whenever possible."

Amy paused. The presenter was fidgeting with a piece of paper, clearly eager to move on to the next award. The audience members looked slightly bored, their eyes glazed by too many speeches and too much wine. At least the bigwigs from her station were smiling at her politely from their table in front. But only because the Emmy would generate more viewers for their station and thereby increase commercial revenues, she concluded cynically.

Suddenly Amy thought of Tony Jackson in Knoxville. There was a man she could admire. His Christian station was in business for the message, not the money. He was committed to doing good work that made a difference in people's lives. The kind of work she liked to do. To him, the money was secondary.

As Amy quickly wrapped up her comments and returned to her table, she felt as if a burden had been lifted from her shoulders. In an instant her doubts and confusion were resolved, and the solution to her dilemma had become clear.

She looked at the statuette in her hand. It was a career milestone, certainly. But more importantly, it was a turning point. Because now she knew exactly what she was going to do.

Cal propped one shoulder against the porch railing and took a sip of his coffee. Autumn was one of his favorite times in the mountains, and he breathed deeply of the fresh, clean scent. There was a nip in the early-November air, and the morning mist still hung over the field in front of the cabin, giving the scene an ethereal beauty. The leaves were a blaze of color on the hillsides, scarlets and oranges and yellows intermingled on a green background, creating a colorful tapestry.

He turned his gaze to the cabin and let it move slowly over the golden logs, still fresh and raw. He'd only moved in a few days ago, but already it felt like home. His part-time law practice was going well, and his job as a ranger was everything he'd hoped it would be. Best of all, he had plenty of opportunity to enjoy the mountains he loved.

Cal knew he was blessed. True, he'd spent a lot of years away from this place, but he'd done good, worthwhile work and, in the end, his time in the city had bought him his dream. He'd invested just about every penny he'd saved in this land and the cabin, but it had been worth it. His needs were simple. And he already had everything he wanted.

Almost.

Cal sighed. His separation from Amy hadn't dimmed his love for her, nor had it eased the ache in his heart. He longed for her with an intensity that produced an almost physical pain. He'd replayed their last conversation over and over in his mind, and each time he felt a renewed pang of regret. She had been right to be deeply hurt by his error of omission. He *should* have told her about his dreams much sooner, just as she'd pointed out. And he *had* discounted *her* dreams. He'd placed her in a position of choosing him or her career, assuming that if she loved him enough, she'd be willing to follow him to the mountains. But he now realized just what a sacrifice he'd asked of her. He didn't doubt her love. She'd demonstrated it to him on every level. And she'd been honest in her feelings and about her priorities. He'd simply chosen to overlook a few key things.

Such as her talent. And her independence. And all the hard work she'd put into her career. And just how difficult it would be for her to continue doing the work she loved in such a remote location.

Bottom line, he'd made some bad mistakes.

He'd also realized something else during these past three months. Much as he loved the mountains, much as they filled a real need in his soul, they couldn't take the place of Amy's love. And so he'd reached a decision. It wasn't the ideal solution from his standpoint, but at least it might be a way around the impasse they seemed to have reached.

Cal took another sip of coffee as he listened to the sound of the nearby stream. It always reminded him of the day he and Amy had hiked to the waterfall, when they'd first acknowledged their feelings for one another. In his mind he could see her just as she'd looked on that day, her eyes tender and filled with longing. He recalled the breathless excitement of their first kiss and remembered the feel of her soft, yielding body in his arms. A surge of desire shot through him, and he steadied his cup with both hands as he drew a deep breath. He'd thought by now that the intensity of his feelings would subside, that the attraction would wane, but just the opposite had occurred. She filled every waking thought, not to mention his dreams, and his need for her grew day by day.

Cal stared out over the meadow, and for just a moment he could almost see her walking up the gravel road to his house, out of the mist, her hair caressed by the gentle breeze, striding with that long, loose-limbed grace that was so much a part of her. It was a scene he imagined every day. Except...

Cal frowned and straightened up. He *wasn't* imagining it! Amy *was* walking up his drive! His heart stopped, then raced on, and he reached out to the support beam, grasping it with a white-knuckled grip. Dear Lord, was he going crazy? Or could this be real?

She didn't seem to be aware of his presence, half-hidden as he was by the morning shadows under the porch, until she was less than twenty feet away. When their gazes did connect, her step faltered and she stopped.

"Amy?" The word came out hoarsely, half question, half incredulous statement.

Slowly she moved forward again, until she was only a few feet away. "Hello, Cal. I hope you don't mind an early-morning visitor." Her words were choppy, and there was a touch of uncertainty in her voice.

His first instinct was to reach out and pull her into his arms, but he hadn't heard from her in three months and he wasn't about to make another mistake by jumping to conclusions. So, with great effort, he restrained himself. "What are you doing here?" he asked cautiously.

Amy tried to smile, but couldn't quite pull it off. "Applying for a job."

He gave her blank look. "What?"

Amy hadn't been sure what reaction to expect from Cal after all this time, but she'd hoped at least for warmth. Maybe more. Instead, he seemed distant. But she wasn't turning around now, even if her stomach was tied in knots and her legs were shaking so badly she was afraid they wouldn't support her weight.

"Is there somewhere we can sit?"

"Sit?" he repeated, still trying to decipher her last statement.

"You know—that thing you do with chairs." Maybe if she tried to lighten the atmosphere a bit he'd loosen up, she thought in desperation.

"Oh…sure. I've only been in here a few days, but

I do have a kitchen set.'' He pushed the door open, and nodded her inside.

Amy had only a fleeting impression of golden log walls, hardwood floors and vast windows as Cal led her to the back of the cabin. ''Would you like some tea?'' His tone was polite, but still cautious.

''Yes. If you don't mind.''

Cal turned away to fill the kettle, willing his erratic pulse to stabilize. He needed a moment to compose himself, plan his course of action now that the woman he loved was actually in his home. Because he didn't want to lose her again. *Couldn't* lose her again.

Amy stared at Cal's broad back as he made her tea, and once more her courage threatened to desert her. What right did she have to barge in here after three months and expect to be greeted with open arms when she hadn't even returned any of his countless calls? What right did she have to think he still felt the same way about her? And what if he *didn't?* Her stomach plummeted to her toes, and she suddenly felt dizzy. She probably should have taken time to eat breakfast, she realized. Especially since she'd skipped lunch yesterday and barely picked at her dinner. But she'd been so anxious to get here. Now she was paying the price. She closed her eyes and willed the world to stop tilting.

''Amy?''

At the sound of Cal's concerned voice, her eyelids flickered open. He was bending down toward her, only inches away, and she wanted to reach out and touch his dear face, smooth away the twin furrows of worry in his brow. But she forced her hands to remain motionless on the table.

"Are you all right? What's the matter?"

"I'm fine." Her voice seemed to come from a distance and sounded faint even to her ears.

"You're not fine. You're pale as a ghost. Are you sick?"

"No." With a triumph of will over body, she forced the world to right itself. But she couldn't do anything about the tremors that ran through her hands.

He hesitated a moment, then sat down across from her, his own hands tightly gripping his mug. He was clearly waiting for her to speak, so she took a deep breath and plunged in.

"Gram told me where to find you. I parked down on the road and walked up because I needed time to gather my courage."

He eyed her warily. "For what?"

She reached into her purse, withdrew a long white envelope with his name on it and laid it on the table. "For this." She took a deep breath a pushed it toward him. "Go ahead and open it."

He gazed at her for a moment, then reached for the envelope and withdrew the contents. The cover letter was addressed formally, and seemed to be a standard job application. He frowned and flipped to the second page. The word *position* was in bold letters, followed by the word *wife*. The next line read, "Top ten reasons why candidate would excel at this job."

Cal scanned the list, a tender smile quirking his lips as he perused it.

10. Good sense of humor

9. Excellent conversationalist

8. Willing to learn how to bake Gram's fabulous biscuits and apple pie—if she is available for lessons

7. Loves children

6. Likes the way you kiss

5. Considers you her hero

4. Is tired of city life

3. Looks forward to living in the mountains

2. Loves you with all her heart

1. Never does anything halfway

The words blurred in front of his eyes when he reached the end of the list, and he blinked a few times before he looked at her. He wanted to accept what she offered at face value, forget about her dreams, but he couldn't. He'd made that mistake once, and he wasn't going to do it again.

"What about your career?"

"I'm resigning from the station in Atlanta."

He shook his head. "I can't ask you to do that. I was wrong to suggest it in the first place."

She reached over and laid her hand on his, her gaze intense and compelling, her voice firm. "I'm resigning, Cal. No matter what happens between us today, I'm moving on. I spent the past couple of days with Tony Jackson in Knoxville, and he's offered me a job. I believe in what he's doing, and he's willing to let me work on the kinds of stories I like best. It's an ideal arrangement."

Cal couldn't doubt the sincerity in her eyes, knew

he shouldn't press his luck, but he had to be sure. "And what about your dreams of a network feature spot?"

Amy shrugged. "It's funny. I worked toward that goal for a lot of years. Pretty much to the exclusion of all else. In fact, at some point the quest became more important than the goal. And then you came along, and suddenly I began to question a lot of things. It wasn't easy to admit that maybe my priorities were out of whack, that somewhere along the way I'd gotten so caught up in the glamour and prestige and power and money part of the business that I'd lost sight of what really counts—doing good work that can help others. I'm not saying you can't do that in a network spot, but I can do it a lot more easily with far fewer personal and ethical sacrifices at Tony's station. And the icing on the cake is that it gives me you, too. Assuming, that is, that you—that you still want me," she finished, her voice faltering.

He studied her in silence for a moment. Then, instead of responding, he rose and retrieved a small envelope from the counter. It was stamped and addressed to her, she noted, as he placed it in front of her. "I was going to mail this today. Open it."

She hesitated, then did as he asked. With her heart pounding, she quickly scanned the single sheet of paper.

My dearest Amy,
Over the past few weeks, as I've settled into the life I always dreamed of, I've discovered one very important thing. Much as I love living in the mountains, my life feels incomplete. I know

now that I can never be truly happy and content here without you by my side. Your love added so much joy and light to my days. Without you, I feel only half-alive.

I know that I hurt you deeply by not sharing my dreams with you. I was wrong to hold them back. Whatever the consequences, I should have told you from the beginning what was in my heart. I only hope you can find it in your own heart to forgive me.

I also know I hurt you by discounting your dreams. Again, I was wrong. You have every right—perhaps even an obligation—to fully develop and use your exceptional talent. But I placed the burden on you to figure out how to do that here in the mountains.

You were right when you said that all the compromises in my original proposal would be on your side. And that's not fair. So I have an idea that may allow us both to pursue our dreams. What if we divided our time between the city and the mountains? Could we find a way to make that work?

What it comes down to, Amy, is this. I love you. And I don't want to spend the rest of my life without you. I'll work with you to find a solution that is acceptable to both of us. Please…forgive me for hurting you, and say that you'll try. Because I count your presence in my life among my greatest blessings, and I love you with all my heart.

As Amy finished the note, her throat grew tight. Cal did still love her! So much that he was willing to compromise his own dream to accommodate hers. He could have given her no greater gift, or demonstrated his love in no more credible or touching way.

"That offer is still open, Amy," he said quietly.

She looked at him, the love shining in her eyes. "And I'll treasure it always. But this is where I want to stay."

Suddenly he took her hand in a warm clasp, then stood and pulled her to her feet. "Come with me," he said huskily.

They retraced their steps through the house to the porch, which was now bathed in golden morning light. He could feel her trembling as he reached over to frame her delicate face with his powerful hands, his thumbs gently brushing her cheeks. He was none too steady himself as he gazed into her beautiful, deep green eyes, misty now, but filled with unmistakable love and tenderness. As his heart overflowed with joy, he suddenly knew that this would always stand apart in his memory as one of the shining, defining moments of his life. A moment he would look back on, in the twilight of their lives, as representative of the dawn of a new day for both of them.

For several seconds they simply gazed at each other, savoring the wonder of their love, filled with hope and joy and the promise of a bright tomorrow. When Cal finally spoke, the catch in his voice tugged at Amy's heart and sent a rush of tenderness through her.

"Three months ago, I planned to bring you to this

meadow and propose on the spot where I wanted to build my home—our home," he said. "I can't promise you that our life here will always be easy, Amy. It certainly won't be glitzy or glamorous. But I can promise you that while our home won't be filled with silver and gold, it *will* be filled with something far more precious—love and friendship and laughter. And I promise you this, too. From this day forward, I will always share with you the secrets of my heart and my dreams. And I'll do everything I can do to help make yours come true. Because I love you with all my heart. Will you marry me?"

Amy's eyes filled with tears, and when she spoke her voice was choked with emotion. "Oh, Cal! You've already made my greatest dream come true. You've given me your love. And you've also helped me find a new life grounded in faith, with a clear sense of what truly matters. For that gift alone, I'll be forever grateful."

His heart soared with joy and his lips curved into a smile as he reached over to gently wipe away a wayward tear that had slipped down her cheek. "Is that a yes?"

A tremulous smile, filled with wonder and anticipation and unbridled joy, lit her face. "That is most definitely a yes," she confirmed.

And as he pulled her into his arms to seal their engagement in the most traditional of ways, Amy said a silent prayer of thanks. For this wonderful man. For this wonderful place. And for a future that she now knew, with absolute certainty, was going to be even more wonderful than the one she had planned.

* * * * *

Dear Reader,

As I write this letter, summer is drawing to a close. Soon I'll put away my gardening tools while the world takes time to rest and renew itself beneath a blanket of snow. I will miss my garden and my woodland retreat, but always I am comforted by the hope and promise of spring.

The hours I spend in my garden are among my most joyous—and most contemplative. And I have learned much—about flowers and about life. Sometimes plants need space so they can grow and fully develop. Sometimes they become weak or vulnerable and do best when close together so that they can prop each other up. Water must be dispensed in just the right proportion—too much, they drown; not enough, they shrivel and die.

Like a garden, love is a balancing act. We must learn when to get close—and when to back off. We must learn how much affection is enough—and how much is smothering. And while we sometimes make mistakes, true love, like a flower, is tenacious. It struggles to survive, even under difficult conditions. Because real love never ends.

In this book, Cal and Amy learn the balancing act of love. They also learn that love sometimes involves difficult choices. But as they ultimately discover, those choices aren't really compromises when willingly made. In fact, love often spurs a healthy realignment of priorities and offers new hope for a better tomorrow, even in times of trouble.

Through all your winter days, may the promise of spring remain in your heart.

Irene Hannon